WILD WEEKEND

WILD HEART MOUNTAIN: WILD RIDERS MC
BOOK ELEVEN

SADIE KING

LET'S BE BESTIES!

A few times a month I send out an email with new releases, special deals and sneak peeks of what I'm working on. If you want to get on the list I'd love to meet you!

When you join you'll get access to all my bonus content which includes a couple of free short and steamy romances plus bonus scenes for selected books.

Sign up here:
authorsadieking.com/bonus-scenes

WILD RIDERS MC

AN INTRODUCTION

Welcome to Wild Heart Mountain home of the Wild Riders MC.

If you love damaged heroes and curvy girl romance, then you'll love the Wild Riders MC.

This group of ex-military bikers fall hard and fall fast when they encounter the curvy women who heal their hearts.

Expect forbidden love, age gap, forced proximity, fake relationships, single dads, single moms and off-limits love with protective heroes who will do anything for the women they love.

Spend some time with Wild Heart Mountain's Wild Riders MC, the MC that's all heart.

Let me introduce you to the members…

Ex-military buddies **Raiden, Quentin and Travis** formed the Wild Riders MC when they got out of the military and wanted to create a place for veterans who love to ride.

They set up their headquarters in a compound on the side of Wild Heart Mountain.

Travis, whose road name is Hops, runs the Wild Taste Bar and Restaurant, and secretly crushes on his best friend's sister.

Quentin, also known as Barrels, runs the award-winning Wild Taste Brewery located out the back of the restaurant. He was a First Class Sargent in the army and you wouldn't want to cross him. Especially where his little sister is concerned...

Colter, or Vintage, is a motorbike mechanic and runs the bike shop. He collects old bikes and loves all things vintage especially the bubbly Danni and her 1950's curves.

Calvin also known as Badge, is the local Sheriff and his uptight views are shaped by loss.

Joseph, or Lone Star is a recluse whose military experiences have given him a distaste for humanity.

Grant goes by Snips. He's the local barber and recently

discovered he has a child. He's learning to navigate life as a single dad.

Arlo earns the road name Prince because of his charming and personable nature. He loves getting under the skin of Maggie, the shy pastry chef.

Davis begins the series as a prospect. Younger than most of the other men, he came out of the military with diminished hearing. His hearing aids make him shy with women and he keeps himself hidden away.

Specs would rather read a book than talk to anyone.

Bit Rate is a grumpy single dad widower in need of a nanny.

Judge is a military lawyer and always does the right thing, until he meets the curvy woman who makes him question his world view.

Luke becomes a prospect after Raiden finds him drinking himself to oblivion in a strip joint. A wheelchair user since he lost both his legs in Afghanistan, Luke finds new purpose with the MC, but can he find love?

Marcus goes by Wood because his family own the local sawmill and it's his medium of choice. He channels his PTSD into his art, creating sculptures that attract the attention of an arts journalist from the city.

On the other side of Wild Heart Mountain is a town called Hope and nestled in the hills is the Emerald Heart Resort. During the summer, it's a popular destination for tourists and in winter, they come for the ski season. Perfect for a snowed in romance…

Stay awhile in Wild Heart Mountain and explore the other series set here.

Wild Heart Mountain: Military Heroes
Wild Heart Mountain: Mountain Heroes
Temptation
A Runaway Bride for Christmas
A Secret Baby for Christmas

WILD WEEKEND

WILD RIDERS MC

A weekend fling, a secret pregnancy, and an ex-military biker who crosses the country to claim his woman.

I don't expect to find a curvy goddess in my motel room shower. And I certainly don't expect her to knock me out with a shampoo bottle.

Our fling begins explosively and ends just as quick.

It was supposed to be one weekend only, but I can't stop thinking about the curvy goddess with the sharp right hook.

But when I cross the country to claim her, Stella's disappeared.

When I finally track her down, she's got a surprise for me.

I'm a man who always does what's right, and I'll do right by Stella.

Until I find out her dark secret and begin to question everything I stand for...

Wild Weekend is Judge's story. A fling turns into love when opposites attract, featuring a secret pregnancy, a curvy girl, and an obsessed ex-military biker who will do anything to claim his woman.

1

WILL

The roar of a thousand motorbikes reverberates off the cliffs like a swarm of angry bees thundering down the highway.

Sunlight glints off the chrome of the hundreds of bikes in front of me, making me squint and doing nothing for my headache.

I look over to the right where Luke rides next to me. His adapted bike has his wheelchair strapped next to him. Luke catches my eye and grins broadly. I force a smile back.

It's good to see him happy, and it's good to see the patch on his jacket. Before we left for the charity run, we voted Luke in as a full member of the Wild Riders MC. He was given the road name Chariot, and seeing him ride his adapted bike with a huge grin on his face, he looks like a Roman warrior returning home. This is his first run with the patch, and he's enjoying every minute of it.

I can't say I share his enthusiasm.

My head aches, my thighs are rubbed raw, and I need a piss. I'm too old for this.

I didn't want to do the charity run in the first place. I've got nothing against the charity. Who wouldn't want to support Women in Need? But it's the other motorcycle clubs here with us that make me uneasy.

Up ahead, I spy an Underground Crows MC patch. They're one of the less savory motorcycle clubs on the charity run. The president has done time, and I'll make sure we steer well clear of them. I don't want any trouble. I want to finish the ride, enjoy the weekend festival, and get the hell back to my quiet mountain.

I've got a list of clients that I need to call. Maxine is handling things back in the office, but I'm the only lawyer on Wild Heart Mountain and I've got a community to serve. So it's with relief that we pass the sign for the Grantstown turn off.

The bikes ahead of us thunder down the off-ramp, and a few moments later we follow.

We ride two by two along the stretch of road, a line of bikers stretching away in both directions. It's an impressive sight, a biker's charity run, as long as you're not a car trying to get past.

We've been on the road for five days. We rode in from North Carolina, and each day we joined with other motorcycle clubs until our cavalcade grew to include most of the clubs from the east coast and the central states. Today we joined up with some clubs from the west coast, and we're rolling into the final destination together.

Grantstown has been taken over for the weekend with a charity festival happening in a field behind the main drag. Every hotel is booked, and a field of tents has been erected for the overflow.

April, Snips's old lady, has handled the planning and got in early to book us a hotel. This biker is too old to camp out in a tent. Besides, I need the internet access to get some work done.

The line of bikers draws to a halt, and I rest my foot on the tarmac. My GPS says we're still a mile out of town, but I guess this is the traffic jam into the event.

The pressure on my bladder is worse with the bike idling, but there's no tree cover, and I'm not going to take a piss on the side of the road with a thousand bikers staring at me.

The flat field next to us does mean I could get an easy run into town. I think about going off road, but then I look over at Luke.

It's his first run, and he's beaming from ear to ear. He left both his legs behind in Afghanistan, and this is the happiest I've seen him since Raiden found him drowning his sorrows in a dodgy strip club.

I glance around, looking for more familiar faces, but in the melee of merging clubs, I can't see any of our other MC brothers. I can't see our patch among the sea of leather.

The Wild Riders MC are veterans who love to ride, and I'm not going to leave one of my MC brothers on his own in this crowd, especially not one as green as Luke. My bladder will have to wait.

Most of the club are grizzly old men like me, but there are a few that are under thirty. Men, that is. There are plenty of younger old ladies since the guys started pairing off like we're in the damned ark.

The line of bikes starts moving, and the effect is like a ripple in the water. From a mile up the road they move first, and five minutes later it's our turn. We creep along at five miles an hour all the way into town.

As we get closer, I spy the first of the townsfolk who have come out to greet us. They line the road on either side for the last quarter mile into town. Some are waving American flags, and others are holding signs in support of Women in Need.

There are plenty of women and children out, and I shelve my discomfort knowing it's for a good cause.

The line of bikes goes straight through the main street in town, and the good cheer is infectious. Despite my headache, aching thighs, and screaming bladder, I smile and wave at the crowd who have come out to witness a thousand bikers invading their town.

Our motel is on the far edge of town, and the parking lot is packed with bikes of all kinds.

Luke gets the only disabled parking space, and I circle twice before pulling in behind him. Bikes are already stacked two or three to a space, and I'll just have to move my bike if Luke wants to go anywhere without me.

I note with annoyance that the Underground Crows MC are staying in the same motel as us. I must remember to warn the guys to keep the hell away from them.

Luke maneuvers himself into his wheelchair and unclips the ties holding it in place. With a push of a lever, a ramp unfolds down the back of the platform and he wheels himself off.

My instinct is to grab his bags for him, but I put my hands in my pockets knowing he prefers to do things for himself. I wait for him patiently, but my bladder is about to explode and I dance from foot to foot.

At that moment Snips comes over with April, and it's a relief to see someone from the club.

"I got your room keys." April holds up two key cards and hands one to Luke. "Yours is on the first floor, and you're sharing with Specs."

Luke takes the key card and wheels off to find his room.

"You're in 102 up top." She hands me the other key card.

"I'm not sharing, right?"

April nods. "Don't ask me how, but I managed to get you a room on your own."

It's a luxury, but I have to work, and I'm too stuck in my ways to share a room with anyone. I paid extra to get a room to myself.

"I owe you a drink."

April smiles and rubs a hand over her pregnant belly. "I'll take a rain check on that."

I shoulder my bag and set off across the parking lot.

"We're in room 107," she calls after me. "And we're all meeting in the bar at five."

I'm already halfway across the parking lot, my

bladder practically bursting with the knowledge that relief is in sight.

I take the stairs two at a time and jog along the walkway until I find room 102. I swipe the key card and push the door open and jog to the bathroom.

All my attention is on my bladder and how quickly I can get to the bathroom. So it's a huge surprise when I push open the bathroom door and find the shower running.

The bathroom is steamed up, and through the mist a flash of skin makes me freeze.

The shower is a see-through cubicle, and inside is a naked woman. She's facing away from me, and I get an eyeful of a delicious curvy ass. She's got soap suds all over her and one arm up in the air as she lathers soap over her voluptuous breasts.

My throat tightens and my heartbeat kicks up a notch as lust races through my veins. There's a stirring down below that's more urgent than the need to pee.

Her hair is dark brown, and water plasters it to her back. The hint of a tattoo peeks through the tendrils, an outstretched paw that belongs to some kind of wild animal.

She slowly turns around, and I'm hypnotized as her breasts come into view. They're full with dusky pink nipples, which she runs a hand over as she lathers soap over her chest.

I should back out of the shower. I've obviously got the wrong room. But I can't move and I can't look away.

I tear my gaze away from her breasts, needing to see her face.

The woman's got youthful skin and full lips and dark brown eyes that widen in horror when she sees me.

Her full pink lips open wide, and she lets out a blood-curdling scream.

I snap back to reality, and I tear my eyes away from the goddess in the shower.

"Get out!" she screams.

I raise a hand to my eyes, shielding them from the glorious sight of her nakedness as I back out of the room.

"Sorry…"

I try to close the door, but she lunges out of the shower wielding a shampoo bottle. Her breasts sway as she goes for me.

Before I can retreat, she attacks. A knee jerks upward, and I move just in time for it to get me in the guts rather than the balls.

I double over at the pain, because she's got a hell of a kick on her. She's a big strong woman, tall and curvy, and there's power behind her swing.

"Get the fuck out of my room!"

I'm doubled over from the kick as she bears down on me with the shampoo bottle.

It strikes me in the temple, and my head swings to the side and hits the side of the door.

The last thing I see is two beautiful breasts swinging in my vision and milky thighs.

Then I hit the floor and everything goes dark.

7

2

STELLA

*T*he pervert hits the floor with one hand clasping his nuts. I give him another bash to the head just to make sure.

I was aware I'd have to keep alert at an event with hundreds of bikers, but I never dreamed one would attack me in my hotel room.

I mustn't have locked the door properly.

My heart's hammering in my chest, and I'm dripping water on the floor. But I need to make sure I've eliminated the threat, then get the hell out of here.

I turn the shower off and grab a towel.

The man groans, and I jump backwards in case he tries to grab me. I've learned out of necessity how to defend myself, and I'm grateful I was able to negate the threat before he tried to do whatever he came in here to do.

But he stays prostrate on the floor. I cautiously shuffle forward to get a better look at him.

The man's got short dark hair and is clean shaven. Not the type of guy you'd pick for a pervert, but then who can tell these days?

There's a trickle of blood on the side of his head where he hit the door. Unease creeps into my stomach. What if I've killed him?

I fight down the panic that threatens.

It was self-defense. He attacked me in the shower. But there were no witnesses, and the last thing I need is to go through the courts again.

I give him a nudge with my foot to check that he's alive. The man groans, and relief floods me.

But if he's alive, I need to get out of here and get some help.

His body is sprawled on the bathroom floor, and I wrap the towel tightly around me and step over him.

In his outstretched hand, he's clasping something that looks like a card of some sort. I crouch down to take a look.

It's a keycard. He's holding a keycard to a motel room, and written on it in black marker is '102'

"Shit."

I grab my keycard from the bed where I chucked it with my stuff and check my room number. It says '102' in red marker.

There's been a room mix up. He didn't come in here to attack me in the shower. He came in here because someone at reception told him this was his room and gave him a key.

"Shit. Shit. Shit."

9

I crouch down and feel his pulse. It's still beating, so that's a good thing. I need to get him into the recovery position in case he's concussed.

He's a big guy and takes up most of the floor in the bathroom. Luckily I'm a big girl and used to moving bodies around from my job as an orderly in an old folks home. What I need is leverage.

I step back over him, aware that with only my towel on if he opened his eyes right now he'd get an eyeful. Although he got a good eyeful a minute ago when I was in the shower.

The thought of this stranger seeing me naked makes my cheeks flame.

I couch behind him and slide my hands under his back. It's a firm back, hard with muscle. I can tell even through the leather jacket he's wearing.

With a heave, I roll him onto his side.

His bikers patch comes into view. The Wild Riders MC North Carolina. He's come a long way. Further than I have from the Sunset Coast of California.

I haven't heard of the Wild Riders, but there must be close to a hundred different clubs on this run.

Up close, I notice flecks of silver in the sides of his dark hair and small lines by the creases of his eyes. He's older than me by at least ten years and handsome now that I know he's not a pervert.

He has a pronounced jawline and mole on the side of his neck. I reach a finger out and press it to the mole. I'm not sure why, I just want to touch him. His skin is olive tanned and smooth. He smells like leather and soap and the dust of the road.

I inhale deeply. It's a nice scent.

The man stirs, and I scramble to my feet. Now I'm the creepy one, crouching over him half-naked and sniffing him.

I step over him quickly and go through to the main room. I call Cleo and ask her to get here quick, but don't tell Kray. If any of the Underground Crows found out a strange man had walked in on me in the shower, they'd deal with it in their own way, and I don't want to be a part of that. Especially since it seems like a mix up with the rooms, rather than a guy sneaking into motel rooms looking for women in the shower.

I hope so, since the guy's hot. And he's seen me naked. The thought makes my skin heat.

I quickly towel off and pull some clothes on, all the while keeping one eye on the man just in case I'm wrong.

A few minutes later, Cleo knocks on the door. She's got Charlie strapped to her chest, and she cradles his head as he sleeps.

I let her in, and her eyes go wide when she sees the man passed out on the floor.

"What the fuck?" Charlie stirs, and I press my finger to my lips.

"Shhhh." I don't want to wake him until I've explained what happened to Cleo.

"Is he dead?" she whispers.

"I don't think so."

"Good. I'd do a lot for you, Stella, but disposing of a dead body is pushing my limits."

I fill Cleo in on what happened, and she shakes her head when I get to the part where I knocked him out.

"Jesus, Stella. Does trouble follow you around?"

I wince at her words because she's right. I've been trying really hard to stay out of trouble, but when it walks right into your bathroom, what's a girl to do?

3
WILL

a vision of two voluptuous breasts dances through my mind. I float between them in a black sea. The blackness holds me down, and I try to swim through it to get back to the breasts and curvy body they belong to.

But they're just out of reach above the surface of the black water. If I can just break through it, I'll see them.

I'm swimming through the blackness and reaching for the breasts...

The vision fades and my eyes flicker open.

The first thing I see isn't breasts but the cold tiles of a strange floor. Female voices reach my ears, and I lift my gaze to see two figures standing together by a bed.

One of them has a child strapped to her front, and the other has her arms folded over her chest.

I try to sit up, and there's a thumping in my head.

"He's awake," one of the women says.

She comes over and crouches next to me. The scent

13

of body wash fills my nostrils, and a memory of being hit by a shampoo bottle makes me wince.

The woman has dark eyes and full lips and she's saying something to me, but I'm mesmerized by her lips moving.

Her dark hair sticks to her shoulders, making her black t-shirt wet. A black t-shirt that hugs her figure and outlines the perfect breasts. She's the woman from the shower. The woman I saw naked. The woman who attacked me.

Her fingers reach for the side of my head, and I recoil. "Are you going to hit me again?"

She winces and presses her lips together. "That depends."

The other woman has come to stand behind her, and she's holding a plastic rattle. But the way she holds it tight in her fist and raised reminds me of the shampoo bottle. A plastic rattle never looked so menacing. "On what?"

"Why are you in my room?"

My key card is still clasped in my hand, and I hold it up to her. "This is my room."

She hurmphs and looks back at the other woman, who raises her shoulders slightly but doesn't lower the rattle.

"I'm in room 102," the pretty woman with the dusky pink nipples says. "There must have been a mix up."

I sit up, and the world goes sideways. Her hands find my shoulders, and she leans me against the wall.

"Take it easy. You've had a knock."

Her voice is smooth like honey and contains nothing to indicate she's the one who's responsible for the knock that has my head thumping and images of dancing breasts going through my mind.

"You attacked me."

She bites her bottom lip. "You walked in on me in the shower."

She's right to be indignant. A strange man just walked in on her naked, her reaction was entirely appropriate.

I shift position and my bladder screams at me, which is a reminder of why I was in such a hurry for the bathroom.

"I need to use the bathroom." She squints at me suspiciously, and I wonder what's got her so jumpy. "I need to empty my bladder, which is why I ran in here so quick. But your attack waylaid me, and now I'd very much like to get on with my bladder emptying."

A ghost of a smile dances on her lips. "You talk funny."

And you have perfect breasts, is what I want to say, but I'm not saying anything provoking. I've seen what she can do with a shampoo bottle.

The woman helps me to my feet, and the room tilts slightly. Damn, I must have really been knocked out.

I stumble, and she catches me. "You need some help?"

There is no universe where a pretty young woman with perfect breasts helps me pee.

I take a breath and steady myself with one hand against the wall. "What are you, a nurse or something?"

She smiles, and it makes her even more beautiful if

that's possible. "Something like that. I work in a nursing home."

Kind and selfless. This woman is more than a perfect set of breasts. But she's still not helping me pee. "I've got this."

A few minutes later with my bladder taken care of, I catch myself in the mirror as I wash my hands. Blood trickles from my temple, and there's a small gash at my hairline.

I need to get cleaned up, then sort out this fuck-up with the room.

When I open the bathroom door, the woman with the rattle is sitting in a chair nursing her baby. She gives me a death stare as if challenging me to say something.

I avert my eyes. I've seen enough breasts today, and even though she's got a muslin cloth draped over her, I don't want to get an accidental look at a boob. Especially as the presence of a baby means there's probably a hairy biker out there somewhere who she belongs to, and the last thing I want this weekend is any trouble.

My attacker is sitting on the bed, and when I turn to her she smiles sweetly at me, and damn but the pain in my head eases a little.

Maybe a little woman trouble wouldn't be so bad.

"Let me look at that for you."

She's got a first aid kit laid out on the bed and retrieves a bowl of hot water from the bathroom. She pulls over the table by the door and sets the bowl on it.

"I'm sorry about hitting you. I thought you were a

pervert. You can't be too careful with all these men around."

I don't blame her. There's got to be at least five bikers for every woman in town right now. It's a family friendly event, and I've seen plenty of kids around. But there are still a lot of single male bikers, and when they're in packs like this, some of them forget how to behave.

Not every MC here is as honorable as the Wild Riders. It was lucky it wasn't one of the Underground Crows that walked in on her. Who knows what those animals would do.

"I can see how it must have looked."

Now that I'm not blinded by the pressure in my bladder, I don't know how I missed the signs of occupation in the room. A black purse is strewn across the bed, and a small duffle bag sits on the table under the television. A pair of bright green sneakers are by the door. In my rush to get to the bathroom, I don't know how I missed them.

The woman dabs a piece of cotton wool in the water and presses it to my forehead. When she leans in her breasts are right by my face, and I catch a whiff of her freshly bathed skin.

I resist the urge to reach out and touch them. I know what they look like under her t-shirt, and that's an image that will stay with me for a long time.

"What's your name?"

"Stella," she says. "And this is Cleo, my sister."

I glance over at Cleo, and she scowls at me. With her heavy eyeliner and all leather outfit, she's a menacing figure. I get the feeling these girls know how to look after themselves.

"I'm Will."

"Nice to meet you, Will."

My name on her lips causes a stir in my pants, and I cover my lap with my hands hoping she doesn't notice. This is the closest I've been to a woman in months, and the heady mix of her scent, her smile, and knowing what her breasts look like has my blood heating.

She works in silence, administering antiseptic, and I give myself over to her soothing hands.

"You've come all the way from North Carolina?"

"How do you know that?"

She leans behind me, and her fingers trace the outline of my patch. "It's written right here."

Her wet hair falls against my cheek, and I capture a strand and twist it around my fingers. Her gaze shifts to my hand, and her mouth pops open in surprise.

"I'm sorry I startled you, Stella."

My eyes dart to her full lips, just inches from mine, and I've never wanted to kiss anyone so bad. Stella's chest heaves up and down, and I think she might feel this connection too.

There's a tiny cough from the corner as the baby finishes it's feed.

I release Stella's hair, and she takes a step back from me. But our eyes remain locked.

"I've put butterfly stitches across the cut. It's not deep, but you'll probably bruise." She bites her bottom lip. "I'm so sorry I did that to you."

It's not convenient having a banging headache and a bleeding head, but I got to meet Stella, so it might even be worth it.

"Don't worry. I'll live. What we need to sort out is where I can get another room."

Stella shakes her head. "Oh no, I can't kick you out after doing this to you. You stay here, and I'll find another room."

We both know there are no other rooms going in town, and if the hotel's fucked up, then the only sleeping space left will be in the field of tents, which is mostly the rowdy singles. There's no way I'm letting this beauty camp down in that nest of vipers.

"I'm not letting you give up your room. I'll find somewhere."

A few minutes later, I've rounded up April who made all the bookings, and we're in the line to speak to reception.

The middle-aged woman behind the desk looks flustered, and I don't blame her. The lobby is filled with angry bikers. It looks like ours wasn't the only mix up.

When we get to the line and explain the situation, she's remorseful but resolute. There are no more rooms.

Stella finds us at reception, and before I can stop her, she hands her key card over to the woman. "He can have the room."

I take her hand to stop her, and a shot of electricity fires up my forearm. Our eyes lock, and her mouth pops open in surprise.

She's the first to recover, and I wonder if it's an effect of the injury making me jumpy.

"It's okay," she says. "There's space in Cleo's room. I'll bed down with them."

"I can't kick you out of your room."

"It's not kicking me out, Will. I don't get much time with my sister. My stuff's already moved."

She glances over at the doorway where Cleo is waiting with the baby tucked into her leather jacket.

"Think of it as compensation for beating you up."

She smiles at me, and I can't resist her infectious grin, but it's not right taking her room. "I'll find a tent to sleep in."

Stella laughs, and it's a deep throaty laugh. "I can't imagine you camping out in the field."

I open my mouth to protest. When I was in the military, I slept rough all the time. But maybe I've gotten soft in my old age as a civilian.

"It's already done. I've moved my stuff, my key's handed in. I promise I won't bother you again."

She turns to leave and I watch her walk towards the door, hoping very much that she does bother me again.

I notice she's not wearing a leather jacket. She doesn't have an old lady patch, which means Stella isn't attached to anyone.

Suddenly, I think a little trouble this weekend might not be a bad thing.

She joins Cleo and holds the door open for her and the baby. As Cleo turns around, I get a glimpse of her biker's patch for the first time.

In emblazoned red letters on the back of her jacket, it reads "Property of the Underground Crows MC."

4

STELLA

The grass squelches under my boots as I trudge through the field, dodging around groups of men in leather. On the far side of the field, a van waves a white flag with Coffee written on it, and that's where I'm heading.

My eyes sting from lack of sleep, and there's a crick in my neck. The trundle bed had a saggy mattress and no pillow. And I was woken several times by Charlie crying and then in the morning by Nina, Cleo and Kray's adopted daughter, jumping on me.

A man steps in front of me, laughing at something his friend said and completely oblivious of his surroundings. I bump into him as he passes, and the stench of stale beer makes me cough.

The men stagger away and I put my head down and keep going, my sole focus the beacon of hope that is the coffee truck.

It rained overnight, and it can't have been nice

sleeping out in the tent area. No wonder they partied into the night. And by the looks of some of them, well into the morning too.

The music carried access the field and into the motel. I could have gone with the other Crows to the party, but I'm not here to court trouble. I preferred to stay in with Cleo and the kids and stay well away from any temptation.

My mind strays to Will, who is the biggest temptation I've seen here so far. But something tells me he wouldn't have been at the party either. He didn't seem like the type to drink in the rain.

Away from the camping area, stalls are set up to sell food and merchandise and other crafts. A stage is at the far end of the field, and at this time of the morning it's all kids' entertainers.

Cleo brought the kids over this morning for the kids' shows, but I got tired of watching a biker in a clown suit and wandered off to look at the stalls.

There's a program of speakers and bands throughout the day culminating in the headline act tonight. But right now, it's coffee I need.

I finally make it across the field and join the long line for the coffee van. The two women behind the counter look harried as they grind beans and steam milk at a furious pace for the needy customers. The delicious smell of freshly brewed coffee hangs in the air. I breathe in deep, and the rich scent puts a smile on my face.

"You look happy this morning."

I jump at the gravelly voice, and the hairs on the back

of my neck stand on end. A shiver zaps down my spine, and I turn to find Will behind me. He's freshly shaved, and his eyes are bright. He looks like he slept well. He looks good, even with the purple bruise around his left temple.

"You scared me." I put a hand over my racing heart, and his eyes dart to my chest then back up to my face.

"I have to stop doing that. I don't want another bruise."

At mention of the bruise, I wince. "I'm so sorry about yesterday."

He frowns at me. "Don't say another word about it."

"How are the butterfly stitches holding?" I reach my hand out to touch his head then hesitate. "May I?"

His eyes lock on mine as my fingers hover over his forehead. They're the deepest brown I've ever seen, almost black.

I didn't realize I'd stepped closer to him, and our faces are only inches apart. I'm tall, five foot nine, and I'm almost eye level with him. I like that Will's taller than me. It's hard finding men who are.

"You may." There's a sparkle in his eyes when he says it, like it's amusing to him.

I carefully slide the hair on his temple back so I can see the wound. There's no fresh blood, and the thin butterfly stitches seem to be doing the job of holding the skin together.

I run my hand over them, and he flinches. "Sorry."

"Stop apologizing, Stella." It comes out as a growl, causing a new wave of heat to course through my veins.

There's a pull low in my belly, and my knees feel wobbly.

"Does it hurt? Do you have a headache?"

"Nothing a strong coffee won't fix. And I took Advil this morning."

"If you go to the local ER, they'll prescribe you something stronger."

"No," he says quickly. "Advil's fine."

I trace the outline of the bruise with my fingertip, enjoying the feel of his skin. His eyes dart to mine, and our gazes lock. My breathing quickens, and heat floods my body. The way he's looking at me like he wants to kiss me makes my core ache.

My lips part on a gasp, and I will him to kiss me. It's been a long time since I felt a man's lips on me, and I've never wanted to be kissed as badly as I do by this man.

"You want a coffee, or what?"

I startle at the woman in the coffee van and step away from Will. I'm back in a muddy field, surrounded by a thousand hungover bikers, and in need of coffee.

"I'll have a double shot with cream and sugar and…" I turn to Will. "What are you having?"

"An americano, no cream, no sugar."

He pulls out his wallet, and before I can protest puts some bills down on the counter. "I got this."

I shake my head. "I should buy you coffee, as an apology for the…" I indicate his head.

Will frowns at me. "You already gave up your room. You can't keep apologizing all weekend."

The woman's already processed the payment and given

25

Will his change. They've got a line of customers behind us, and she has no time for us quibbling about who pays.

We wait at the other end of the truck while the second woman makes our coffee. Will turns to me with his hands in his pockets.

"You're with the Underground Crows." He says it as if he's sucking on a lemon, like the Crows are something distasteful.

"Cleo's husband Kray is a Crow."

Will's frown deepens. "You involved much with the club?"

There's disapproval in his voice that gives me pause. He's part of an MC too, so I'm not sure what he's getting at.

"I've spent some time at the clubhouse since I've been staying with Cleo. They're good guys."

Will grunts, and a flash of something passes across his face. Is that jealousy? That can't be right. We only just met.

"They can't be that good of guys if the President spent three years inside."

The heat drains from my face, and I look down at my hands. I have a small ring with a rose pattern, and I twist it in my fingers.

"That was a long time ago," I say quietly, hoping he doesn't notice the strain in my voice. "They've gone legit. All their business is above board."

"How do you know that?"

I sneak a look up at Will. He's clean cut and well-groomed and has probably never done anything he regrets in his life. Which is the opposite of me.

I have no business being attracted to a man like him. I'll get my coffee, and then I'll go and ignore this connection between us.

"Because Cleo takes in foster kids. They had a full report done on her and Kray. Cleo wouldn't stick around if Kray was into anything dodgy."

"You have a lot of faith in your sister."

She has a lot of faith in me is more like it. Cleo was always the one with the kind heart and resolve of steel.

The woman hands over our coffees, and I wrap my hands around the warm cup.

"I don't believe people just change like that." Will isn't letting it go.

"You don't think people can change? You don't think people deserve a second chance?" I hold my breath, waiting for his answer.

"With a good reason, perhaps. But most people don't change."

I take a sip of my coffee, taking in his words. In the clean cut world he comes from, perhaps people don't change. But I believe in second chances. I've had one myself.

Will's face lights up, and I follow his gaze.

On this side of the field is a row of carnival games. In the stall on the end, a large man with an American flag emblazoned on his leather jacket is handing over three balls to a gangly kid.

"You want a try at the coconut shy?" The disapproving look is gone, and Will is relaxed and smiling.

I should walk away; I have no business being attracted to a man like Will. But his smile is infectious, and instead of walking away, I follow him to the coconut shy.

Will buys us each a turn and hands me the first ball. He holds my coffee while I take aim at the coconut.

The first one goes too far left, and I try again. The second one misses, and the third skims the coconut but it doesn't fall. "So close!"

"But not close enough," the man running the stall croons.

"Let me try." I hold the coffees while Will takes the balls.

He half crouches as he assesses the angle. Then he plants one foot in front of the other and takes his time aiming. I use the opportunity to watch him.

He's tall, at least six feet, and his shoulders are broad. Under his leather jacket, he wears a tight white t-shirt that shows off a muscular chest.

He fixes the coconut with a look of determination, taking his time to focus. I wonder what it would be like to have his attention focused on me. A delicious shiver runs down my spine.

His hands are big and strong, and I bet he knows how to use them on a woman. The hairs on my arms stand on end thinking about it. It's been far too long since a man got close to me. And now my body is going crazy for the first good-looking one who pays me attention.

I need to get a grip. Or maybe I need to let go. I'm not sure which.

Will throws the ball and it skims the coconut. The coconut wobbles and drops to the ground with a thud.

He takes his time with the next one, adjusting his stance. This time he knocks it clear off the stand.

I cheer, and the man behind the stall scowls. I take it he doesn't like people to win.

Will throws the next ball, and the next coconut falls to the ground. He turns to me, grinning, and the smile is infectious.

"Choose any of the prizes on the left," the man mutters.

"Which one do you want?" Will asks me.

"Me?" The prizes are oversized stuffed animals, the kind of thing Cleo's kids would love. "Don't you have anyone you want to give it to?"

He fixes me with an intense look that makes the back of my knees tremble. "Yes. You."

His eyes are dancing, and when he looks at me like that my panties dampen and I squeeze my thighs together.

I quickly turn back to the stall owner. "I'll take the giraffe." Nina will love it.

He hands over the giraffe, and now I've got this big thing to lug around with me. We continue down the stalls, stopping to play each carnival game.

Will is easy to talk to and he's good at these games, especially the shooting ones.

"Where did you learn to shoot?" I ask after he knocks down three yellow duckies in a row with an air rifle.

"I was in the military."

That doesn't surprise me. There's something about the clean cut biker that screams military. Except he doesn't talk like a soldier.

I'm about to ask which regiment he was in when Will's eyes light up. "Whack-a-mole. I bet you're good at this one," he teases.

He's right. I'm a little too vigorous at smashing the mallet down on the poor moles. But it's the only game I win my own prize at.

By the time we come to the end of the line of carnival games, my arms are full of stuffed animals, a bag of candy floss, and a rainbow slinky.

All of them are prizes that Will insisted I take. I'll give them all to Cleo for the foster kids that stay with her sometimes.

As we near the beer tent, the crowd thickens and the sounds of rowdy men talking fill the air. In front of us, a man pushes another guy from a different club who stumbles back into a group of men.

I stop, and Will stops with me. I don't want to go anywhere near trouble, and this doesn't look good.

"Do you want to get out of here?" Will asks.

I peer at him over the head of a stuffed bear. I've just spent an hour with him, but it doesn't feel like enough. "Where to?"

"Let's go for a ride. Away from this."

It's like he read my mind. The thought of the open road with him by my side makes me grin. "Let's do it."

5

WILL

*H*alf an hour later, after depositing the stuffed animals at the hotel and grabbing sandwiches and fruit for a picnic, I'm riding along the highway with Stella on her bike next to me.

Her leather riding jacket is worn, and there's a patch sewn over a hole in the elbow, but there's no club patch on it.

She's not wearing anything to indicate she's part of the Underground Crows. I don't believe for a second that they've gone legit. People don't change, and I don't like the idea of Stella hanging out with them.

But I've not felt a pull like this to a woman for a long time, so I'm not going to dismiss her by association. If she's with the Crows, then she's from the West Coast, so there's no harm in spending time with her this weekend.

Stella looks good in leather. I haven't been able to get the image of her naked in the shower out of my head. I know what she's got under her t-shirt, but it's not just the image of her breasts that make me want to spend time with her. Stella is fun to be with. She smiles easily, and I like making her laugh.

We ride away from the town, from the rowdy men and the muddy field. I lost my MC brothers somewhere in the beer tent, but no one will miss me for a few hours.

The wind of the highway whips against my cheeks, my bike thrums under my thighs, and I've got a beautiful woman riding beside me. It's a fantastic feeling, despite being saddle sore. I'll take this any day over being back in that field.

I turn to look at Stella, and she's grinning. The smile makes my loins tingle. I don't know what it is about this girl, but she's got my body on fire.

I checked out the local geography, and there's a small wood with walking trails not too far from here. I miss the wooded mountain, and I need to see some green after riding through arid landscapes for the last few days.

We take the next off ramp, and I lead us down a gravel road. Pine trees thicken above us as the road takes us deeper into the wood. It's quiet out here. No cars pass us, and there's nothing but the thrum of our bikes, a good respite from the chaos back at the festival.

We come to the end of the road, and there's a little parking lot. No other cars are here, and we park the bikes. Wooden markers indicate walking trails, and I choose a short three kilometer loop trail.

I don't know if Stella likes walking or not, but I just want to be near her and away from anybody else.

I grab my backpack from the back of the bike and a

picnic blanket that I always keep in my saddle bag, and we set off down the trail.

"Do you hike much?" Stella asks.

I grab Stella's hand, and she links her fingers through mine. Warmth spreads through me at her touch. "We've got good trails around Wild Heart Mountain. I don't know anybody who doesn't hike."

"What's it like, North Carolina? I've never been there."

There's a whimsical note to her voice, and I wonder about this woman that I know so little about. "It's beautiful."

As we walk through the towering pine trees, I tell Stella all about Wild Heart Mountain, the beauty of the forest, the trees and the rivers and lakes.

I tell her about the Wild Riders MC clubhouse nestled on the side of the mountain with a restaurant and a brewery and a bike repair shop.

She listens intently with a look of longing on her face. I get the feeling she hasn't travelled much and never to that side of the country.

The path meanders to the left, but there's a clearing to the right that looks perfect for our picnic.

"You hungry?"

"Starving."

We head off the path to the right, weaving through thick trees until we come to the clearing.

I shake out the picnic blanket, and we sit down on the forest floor. The only sounds are the birds and the soft breeze as wind ripples the leaves of the trees.

I unwrap the picnic and hand Stella a chicken sandwich.

We eat as we talk, and when the sandwiches are done, I pull out two bananas. "It was the only fruit they had at the stall."

She takes one, and as she bites into it my gaze is drawn to her mouth. Her lips are full and pink, and when they wrap around the banana my cock jerks awake. It's as if those lips are around my dick, and I can feel every caress.

I've had a semi ever since I saw Stella naked, and bringing bananas for a picnic was a bad idea.

"Are you okay?" There's real concern in her voice, and I must be staring at her.

I look away and sit up to hide my boner. Why the fuck did I bring bananas?

A cool breeze ripples across my arms, and it's a welcome relief from the heat that's scorching my body.

"Yeah," I mumble.

A large raindrop falls on my cheek, and I squint up at the sky. Dark rain clouds hang above us. They must have closed in while we walked. Another raindrop hits my face, then another. "Fuck, it's raining."

We spring to our feet at the same time. Stella gathers the empty food wrappers and stuffs them in the backpack while I grab the blanket.

The shower hits hard and fast, and in a matter of seconds the raindrops have turned into a deluge.

Stella shrieks as the rain soaks her skin. It turns into a

laugh as she runs for cover under the nearest tree. I follow her, stuffing the picnic blanket into the backpack.

The thick branches of the tree protect us from the sudden down downpour, but Stella's already wet. Her hair clings to her cheeks, and water glistens on her leather jacket.

She's laughing, and it's infectious. Everything about this woman gives me a warm feeling. With her eyes sparkling and droplets of water sitting on her hair, she takes my breath away.

Rain splashes on my back, and she pulls me closer under the tree. "You're getting wet."

She's leaning with her back against the trunk, and I'm so close I can smell her shampoo.

"You didn't tell me where you were from."

She looks away, and it's a few more moments before she answers. "I've been staying with Cleo on the Sunset Coast."

I had gathered that much, but I notice she says where she's staying but not where she's from.

The Sunset Coast is in California, on the other side of the country from North Carolina. We couldn't get more distant.

"The other side of the country, huh?"

"Afraid so." Stella looks up at me, and she's so close the heat of her breath skims my lips. My heart races, and I've never wanted to kiss anyone so much as I want to kiss her.

I barely know her, and she lives so far away from me. But I can't help myself. "So it would be crazy to do this."

My lips brush hers. It's barely a touch, but heat zings through me from the contact.

My fingers cup her chin, and she looks up at me with wide eyes. She's breathing hard and her chest is heaving up and down, so tantalizingly close.

"Crazy," she whispers.

Her eyes dart to my lips and back to mine. She wants this as much as I do.

I press my lips to hers, and they part for me. Her body shudders, and my hand slides behind her head.

Sparks fly through my body at the contact. She's soft and warm, and this one kiss has my body on fire and my dick lengthening.

The rain pounds the ground around us with the occasional drop making it through the canopy of trees.

When I pull back, her eyes are deep pools of desire. I've never met a woman who turns me on so much. "And it would be even more crazy to do this."

My hand slides between her legs, and I stroke her sensitive parts through her leather pants.

"Yes," she pants. "Utterly crazy."

Stella's back arches, and her hips jut forward. She moans at my touch, and the sound goes straight to my dick.

Ever since I saw her naked, I've wanted her, and my body trembles with anticipation.

I kiss her throat as I stroke her, planting kisses on her wet skin. She tastes of raindrops and the forest and that damn floral scent that drives me wild.

"I want you, Stella." I nip at the skin below her ear, eliciting a whimper.

"I want you too."

The blood rushes straight to my dick, and I have to refrain from ripping her clothes off like I want to.

I pull away and look at her. She's breathing hard, her eyes dark. A vision of beauty as the rain pelts down around us. "This can't lead anywhere, you know that?"

Disappointment flashes across her face before she masks it with a smile. "I realize that. I'm not planning to move to North Carolina anytime soon."

The thought of Stella on Wild Heart Mountain makes my breath hitch. An image of her at the club, by my side, pops into my brain, and I shake it away. It's an impossibility.

"It's impossible. But I like you, and we're both here for the weekend…"

She takes my hand and places it on the zipper of her jacket. "Just for the weekend, Will. I'm fine with that."

I unzip her jacket with trembling fingers, wondering briefly if I'm okay with that.

But all thoughts of the future flee my mind when I unzip Stella's jacket. Her breasts are pushed up against a bright yellow t-shirt that looks too small for her.

I already know what they look like, but I have to feel them, to taste them.

My hand slides up her t-shirt and closes over her left breast. I pull the bra down and sink my fingers into the soft flesh, groaning at the heavenly feel of her breast in my hand.

"I haven't been able to stop thinking about your breasts since I saw you in the shower."

Stella giggles. "Do you want to see them again?"

I let out a long sigh. "Oh yeah."

She shrugs her leather jacket off, and it falls to the ground. Her eyes dance as she tugs her t-shirt over her head.

She's wearing a black lace bra and her breasts burst out of the top of it, too big to be contained.

My breath hitches. She's beautiful, tall and curvy and giving me the sexiest smile.

She reaches behind to unhook her bra, but I stop her hand. "I want to do that."

She's so fucking hot and I want her so bad that if I see her naked now, I might lose it in my pants. Also, I want to please Stella first. This may just be for the weekend, but I want to treat her right.

My dick's painful in my pants, but I can wait.

I put one hand on the tree trunk and push Stella back so she's leaning against the bark. "Are you warm enough?"

She catches her bottom lip in her teeth and gives me a sexy smile. "I will be."

My hand slides over her pale skin, enjoying the feel of her soft belly. I kiss her neck and her throat, and when I reach her breasts, I pull the bra down.

The dusky pink nipples pop out, and I take one in my mouth. She gasps as I swirl the peak around my tongue.

I reach for the other breast and give it the same attention. My hands unclip her bra, and it falls to the floor.

I take my time exploring her breasts, cupping them in my hands and sucking on the nipples. She moans and leans her head against the tree.

A thick raindrop lands on her breasts, and I lap it up with my tongue. With my other hand, I undo her pants and slide my hand inside.

She gasps as my fingers graze her panties. They're soaking wet, and it's not from the rain.

"You want me to make you come?"

Stella whimpers at my words, and I slide my hand under the cotton of her panties.

"Will." She moans at the contact as I slide my fingers between her slick folds. Her scent catches on the wind and makes my dick ache.

The rain is relentless, and even sheltered we're getting dripped on. But the cool splash of rain helps to ease my heated skin.

My hand strokes Stella's most sensitive spot while I nip and suck at her breasts. She gives in to me, trusting me completely with her body.

My finger edges into her, and she cries out. She's so tight, and that makes my dick twinge. I long to feel her around me and I let my hand prime her body for me, getting her ready to take my dick.

The animal inside me gets impatient as I work her sweet pussy. Then she clamps around my fingers, and her head knocks against the trunk of the tree. She cries out as she comes, and her juices coat my fingers.

She pants hard, and I want to make her scream like that again, but this time with me inside her.

I loosen my jeans and shrug out of them, discarding them on the forest floor. My fingers tug at Stella's remaining clothes, and I pull her pants and panties off in one impatient sweep.

Now she's completely naked, and if I don't get inside her soon, I'm going to explode right here.

"Fuck." I slap my hand to my forehead, and Stella looks startled. "I don't have a condom."

She's panting hard, and if I can't fuck her, I'll explode all over her.

"I'm on the pill," she says. "And I'm clean."

It's a risk, but I need to be inside this woman. "Are you sure?"

I stroke my dick, and she looks down at it and licks her lips. "I'm sure. We're safe."

"I'm clean too." I don't want to admit how long it's been since I've been with a woman. Too long if the way my dick's about to detonate is any indication.

"Turn around." It comes out as a growl.

Stella does what she's told, and I push her back down so she's bent over. She wraps her arms around the back of the tree and throws me a saucy look over her shoulder. Her hair whips across her back, and she looks so damned sexy.

I grab her hips and position myself between her thighs. "Spread your legs."

She does as she's told, and I nestle in closer. My cock slides between her slick folds, and it already feels so fucking good.

Her fingers slide between her legs and she directs me to her pussy, as impatient for this as I am.

The tip edges in, and a shiver runs through me as my entire body springs to life. "Brace yourself."

It's all the warning I give her before I slam into her pussy, sinking myself deep into her warm space.

"Will!" she cries out, and her body bucks forward. I grab her hips and pull her back on my cock, sliding her down my shaft.

"Good girl, Stella," I coax her. "Take my dick like a good girl."

She moans and her hips ride back, pushing into me and taking me deeper.

"You like that?"

"Yes," she whimpers.

"Good."

I reach forward so I'm leaning over her and grab her breasts in both hands. My fingers flick the nipples, and she cries out. But I can't get as deep as I want to go. I want to sink right into Stella and give her everything I've got.

Rain splashes through the trees, coating her body in water. Droplets splatter on her bare skin, and my hands slip as I grab her hips.

Stella's face presses into the bark as I ride her hard. I've imagined this all night long, ever since I saw her naked, and now I'm enjoying every part of Stella.

But I want her to enjoy it too. "Touch yourself."

She slides a hand between her legs and moans as she

rubs her pussy. Her fingertips graze my balls, making me cry out.

She throws me a look over her shoulder that's all sex. "You like that?"

"Fuck."

She smiles and scratches her fingernails down my balls.

"You keep doing that, and I'm going to lose it."

"Good," she says. "Lose it, Will."

"Fuck." I grunt with every thrust. What I need is to bury myself deep in this woman again and again. And I do, pounding her so hard that her face scratches against the side of the tree.

Her movements become more vigorous and her moans higher pitched. My balls pull up tight as her pussy tightens around me. Stella climaxes, and I let myself go with a loud groan.

The orgasm explodes out of me, sending shock waves through my entire body. Waves and waves of pleasure emanate from my dick, sending my seed deep inside Stella. I cling on to her hips and shout into the rain.

I've never come so hard in my life, and I stay inside her until every last drop is drained.

It takes a long time for the climax to subside, and when it does, I spin her around and pull her into my arms. "Are you okay?"

It was rough and urgent, and she probably deserves better.

But aside from a few scratches on her arms and one

on her cheek from the bark, Stella's smiling up at me. "I'm hungry."

I kiss her delicate nose and her wet hair.

"Come back to my hotel room. Stay with me tonight." I'm already imagining all the things I want to do with Stella, all the ways I want to explore her body.

She smiles up at me and doesn't hesitate for a moment. "Okay."

She leans into me, and her wet hair falls on my chest. I sweep it out of the way with my fingers, wondering if one weekend with Stella will be enough.

6

STELLA

"*A*re you sure you want to stay in his room?" Cleo asks me for the tenth time.

I think about what we did under the tree this afternoon, and my body heats at the memory. I want more of that.

I've never felt so alive as when Will made love to me, if you can call what we did making love. It was more urgent than that. It was pure lust and desire, and I want to do it again.

I didn't tell him that I'd never gone all the way with a man before. He might have stopped. He might have been gentler, and that's not what I wanted.

"Definitely." I can't keep the smile off my face, and she smiles with me.

"Just be careful." Charlie gurgles, and she jiggles him on her hip. "And use protection."

Cleo always kept an eye on me in the foster home. She's the closest thing to a sister I've ever had. We were

45

only together for two years, and I missed her like crazy when she left.

Cleo was always the sensible one. She kept me in line and made me think twice about the consequences of my actions. I didn't get into any trouble when she was around. But when she aged out of the system and left the Mackeys, I had no one to keep me in check.

I often wonder if the trouble that came after that would have happened if Cleo had still been around.

"I'm on the pill."

"Good." Charlie wails, and she furrows her brow and puts the back of her hand to his forehead. "And Kray has to meet him."

I roll my eyes, even though I'm grateful that she's being protective like a big sister. But I don't want Will to have second thoughts.

I like talking to Will, and I definitely like what else we do together. But when Cleo gets determined about something, there's no stopping her.

A few moments later, I knock on the door to room 102.

"Is this really necessary?"

Behind me stands not only Kray but Lyle and Jesse too, three of the biggest members of the Underground Crows MC. With their leather jackets and grim looks, I'll be lucky if Will doesn't run for the hills, especially with what he said this morning about not believing they've gone legit.

He pulls open the door and doesn't even flinch when he sees the men standing behind me.

"Sorry," I say as Will eyes the men. "They insisted on meeting you. This is Kray, Cleo's husband."

"Your brother-in-law."

Kray doesn't correct Will. We're not blood related, but the MC is like a family, and since I've been staying with Cleo, they've taken me in as their own.

"Come in, gentlemen."

Will steps back and opens the door wide. Relief sags my shoulders, and I turn to the Crows. "They don't need to come in," I say pointedly. "They just wanted to meet you."

But Kray is already striding into the room. He eyes Will warily, and Jesse cracks his knuckles.

They're doing the intimidating thing when I know they're a bunch of softies underneath. I watched Kray change a diaper five minutes ago, and Lyle took his baby girl out for a walk this morning so his old lady could have a sleep in.

"What club are you from?" Kray asks.

Will turns around so they can see the patch on his jacket. "The Wild Riders. We're based in North Carolina."

"I've heard of the Wild Riders," Lyle pipes up. "You're the veterans with the brewery."

"That's right."

Lyle grins, all pretense of being a hard-ass evaporating. "I was in for twelve years. Special Ops."

Lyle is ex-military same as Will, and that seems to boost his esteem in the men's eyes.

Will nods respectfully. "JAGs."

"You don't say? Did you see action?"

"Afraid so. Posted in Afghanistan for a long time."

The men talk military, and the tension eases in the room. It's another ten minutes before I'm able to hustle them out of the door.

Kray hands me my overnight bag. "You change your mind, you know where we are." He gives Will a pointed look. "She comes to any harm, and we'll come back and rip your balls out."

Then they're gone and I close the door behind them and lean against it, wondering if Will has changed his mind.

"Are all bikers so overprotective?" I've only been staying with Cleo for a few weeks, but I get the feeling Kray really would rip his balls out.

Will looks amused. "I wouldn't expect anything less. They look out for their own. I guess they can't be all bad," he admits reluctantly.

"I don't need anyone looking out for me," I mumble, even though that's not true.

Will saunters over to where I'm leaning against the door. "Can I expect any more threatening visits? An angry boyfriend?"

I shake my head and he plants a hand either side of me, boxing me in. "I'm all yours." Just for the weekend, I remind myself.

My breath hitches as Will leans close enough to catch his scent. He's fresh out of the shower and smells of masculine body wash and leather. "I like the sound of that."

His lips press against mine, and the kiss makes me

forget about the Crows and Cleo and anything else but the warmth that passes through my body.

He's got me pinned against the wall, and his body brushes against mine. Heat fizzles through me, and my core tightens. I slide my hands around his back and pull him closer. My hips grind against him, needing the friction.

My jacket is hanging open, and Will runs a hand up my body to palm my breasts. It's only been a few hours since our session in the woods, but my body responds to him with a need so strong I can't deny it. I don't want to deny it.

I try to do what the therapist taught me and run through the consequences in my head before taking action. But the overwhelming need for this man pushes out any thoughts of consequences. I need to feel my skin against his skin and to feel him inside me again.

I pull his jacket off his shoulders and down his arms. He shrugs it off, and it drops to the floor. My fingers run down his t-shirt and over his hard torso. But I need to feel what's underneath.

My thumbs hook under his t-shirt. "Take this off."

Will raises an eyebrow at me. "Impatient much?"

I giggle because I've never felt like this about a man before.

Previously I put up with kisses and fumbles, trying to convince myself I liked it. But I always stopped short of going all the way. This is the first time with a man where I'm the one who can't keep my hands off him.

I tug at his t-shirt until it's over his head, and his bare

muscular chest ripples before me. My mouth goes dry as I trace my fingers over the hard ridges of his body.

Inked designs curl over his shoulders, and he has a small scar by his chest. Before I can explore, he tugs at my t-shirt, and I lift my arms so he can pull it off.

Cool air skims my body. Will slides a hand around my back and unhooks my bra. My breasts tumble out, and he catches them in his hands.

I've always hated my oversized breasts. They attract too much attention, but for the first time, I like that attention.

Will treats them like they're precious parts of me to be worshipped. There's a reverence in the way he traces his fingers around my aureola, making me shudder with the sensation.

I do the same with his torso. It's the first time I've seen him without a t-shirt, and his body is a hard wall of muscle.

My fingertips trace a tattoo that starts at his shoulder and winds down his chest. There are tiny hairs around his nipples, and I tug them with my fingers. Will takes a sharp intake of breath, and I glance up at him in wonder.

"You like that?"

He smiles down at me lazily. "Very much."

I press my lips against his sensitive nipples, and he shudders. I've found his sensitive spot, and my tongue laps at one nipple while my finger traces the other.

Will groans, and I love the sounds he makes. I want to make him groan like that again and again.

His hands tangle in my hair, and he lifts my head up.

"You keep doing that, and this will end before it's started."

That makes me giggle, because I can't imagine this strong man being brought to his knees by his nipples.

A surge of warm emotion runs through me. He's vulnerable just like anyone else.

Will's hands unzip my pants, and he pulls them down my legs so all I'm wearing are my cotton panties.

I showered when we got back to the motel, rain-soaked and happy. And I put on my best underwear. But even my best has a hole in the side.

I slide them down with my pants, not wanting him to see. When I step out of my underwear, I'm completely naked.

Will runs his eyes over me, and the heat in them makes my nipples harden.

I tug at his pants and crouch before him, sliding them down his legs. His cock sticks straight out in front of me, and I press my lips to the tip.

It jerks at me, and Will groans. But he takes my shoulders and pulls me to my feet.

"I want to be inside you, Stella."

The words fill me with heat, and suddenly the urge to feel him in me is overwhelming. He must feel it too, because he kisses me hard and pushes me up against the back of the door.

His hand slides between my legs, and sweet pleasure fills me at his touch. His mouth caresses my breasts, and it's too much.

"Will!" My fingernails dig into his shoulder as the

51

orgasm hits, unexpected and strong. I cry out as it crashes over me making me shudder.

Will presses his palm against me until my pussy stops convulsing. "You okay?"

I'm not okay. This man makes me come undone with the slightest touch, and still I'm not satisfied.

"No." I shake my head, and he freezes. "I want you, Will. I need you inside me."

"I can help with that."

He hoists one of my legs up, and his hardness searches for me. I adjust my stance until his tip finds what it's searching for. I gasp at the sensation as he eases into me. The fullness feels so good I forget to breathe.

We move in rhythm, our hips sliding against each other and our bodies slick with sweat.

He lifts my other leg and hoists me onto his hips, and I lean against the door as he slides me onto his length, with every thrust going deeper until I'm so full of him I can't think of anything else.

The pressure builds, and I cry out. But Will doesn't relent with his pace. He slams me against the door, making the doorframe rattle. My cries fill the room and anyone walking past will hear us, but I don't care.

All I care about is the sensations of this man filling me up, making me whole.

"I'm going to come," I cry, and before I get the words out my world explodes.

I shatter against Will, crying his name as wave after wave of the deepest pleasure I've ever experienced hits my body.

Will slows enough for me to ride out my climax, then he picks up the pace again, thrusting harder and grunting every time he slams into me.

My fingers dig into his shoulders, and I fall over the edge again.

"Will!"

This time he comes with me, shouting my name and slamming so hard I think we're going to go right through the door.

I'm panting hard, and my emotions are flying around so intensely that I need something to cling onto.

I sag against him with my pussy throbbing.

"You okay?" he asks.

It takes me a moment to get my emotions under control enough to answer. I've never felt these sensations before, and it's terrifying. "Yeah."

He carries me to the bathroom and sets me down on a stool. "Let me clean you up."

Will runs a washcloth under the hot water and crouches before me. He runs the washcloth up my thighs, clearing away the stickiness of our combined juices.

He does one thigh and then moves onto the other, carefully wiping the warm cloth up my leg. No one has ever taken care of me like this before. I watch him quietly, this strong man kneeling before me. This is what it must be like to have a boyfriend who cares for you.

I shake the thought out of my head. This isn't a boyfriend situation. We live on opposites sides of the country. Will made it clear this is a fling for this weekend only. I can't expect anything else.

7

STELLA

*E*arly morning light filters into the motel room through the flimsy curtains. A heavy arm drapes across my hip, and Will's thigh presses into the side of my leg. Sometime in the night we gravitated toward each other, our bodies exhausted from the love-making sessions.

After he took me against the door, we ordered take out and stayed in the motel room missing the bands and the speakers.

I didn't mind. We made love bent over the chest of drawers and again in the shower. My body can't get enough of Will.

I'm sore in places I didn't know you could be sore. But it's a good sore, like how athletes must feel after running a marathon.

I watch Will sleep, noting the permanent creases in his forehead and the tiny silver hairs that streak his hairline. He's had worries in his past, concerns that have lined his face.

Will's eyes flicker open, and I close mine quickly so he doesn't catch me staring at him.

"Good morning." His voice is raspy, and it sends a delightful shiver down my spine.

When I open my eyes again he's smiling at me, causing little creases to form in the corners of his eyes. "Morning."

This is the closest we've been except for making love, and I wonder if he's going to pull away from me. But instead he stretches his arm around me and pulls me closer.

I rest my head on his chest and listen to his heart. The thumps slow and steady and I close my eyes, enjoying the solidness of having someone to hold.

Will kisses the top of my head. An intimate gesture, too intimate. I sit up before I lose myself in him completely.

"What did you do in the military?" I bunch the pillows up so I'm sitting and pull the blankets over my chest.

"I was a JAG captain."

He must see my confusion, because he explains. "An attorney, a military lawyer."

My heart skips a beat. Will is a lawyer. It doesn't surprise me with his clean-cut looks, but it's still a shock.

"Is that what you do now?"

He props himself up on one elbow and traces the line of my arm with his fingertip. "I've got a practice in Hope.

It's a small town on Wild Heart Mountain near where I live. I have local civilian clients, but I also take military cases still."

He tells me about his work and I nod and smile along, but my heart is sinking. He's a good guy, a right side of the law kind of good guy, which is more than I am. It's lucky this is only a fling. That he's only mine to enjoy for a weekend.

"What do you want to do today?" he asks, oblivious to my thoughts.

My body tingles thinking about all the things I want to do to Will today, but I need to give my body a rest.

"Don't you have things organized with your club?"

Will puts his arm around me and pulls me back to his chest. "I was going to ride back today, but I think I'll stay another night."

He runs his fingers through my hair. It's soothing, and I could stay here all day listening to his heartbeat and forgetting about the different lives we lead.

"I'd rather spend the day with you."

The words make me feel warm all over even though he must just mean to have sex. "I'm a little sore…"

His fingers move to the front of my scalp and make their way back through my hair. "I mean go get breakfast, see the sights."

"What sights are there to see in the middle of a bikers festival?"

He reaches for his phone. "Let's find out."

. . .

A few hours later, we're wandering the streets of a small town that's a twenty minute ride from where the festival is.

The streets are lined with motorbikes from festival goers who have had the same idea.

We stopped for ice cream at a local store, and I clasp my cone in one hand and Will's hand in the other.

"Have you always lived in North Carolina?"

I take a lick of my strawberry ice cream, and Will's eyes dart to my mouth. The look he gives me makes my body heat, and I lick the ice cream again just to see that look again.

"I moved there after my parents died."

I jolt to a stop, all thoughts of provocative ice cream licking fleeing my mind. I know what that loss feels like.

"I'm sorry, Will. How old were you?"

He squeezes my hand, and I start moving again. "It was a long time ago. I was seventeen. I went straight into the military."

We pass a trash can and I throw the rest of my ice cream in, no longer hungry. "Is that where you studied to be lawyer?"

He nods. "The military trained me, and I threw myself into my studies. My father was a military lawyer with the JAGs, and I wanted to do him proud. I was driven. Too driven."

The last bit he mutters and turns away as he says it. I wonder what haunts him, but I'm too caught in my own thoughts to ask.

"I lost my parents too."

Will stops walking and turns to me. "I'm so sorry, Stella. How old were you?"

It's been a long time since I talked about this voluntarily. My therapist made me talk about my past, and I'm getting better at it. For years I kept it bottled up, and it still feels weird to talk. But Will's looking at me like he really cares, like he wants to know.

"My dad left when I was two. Mom tried to track him down. We moved around a lot, but when she finally found him, she was too late. He was dead."

I don't tell Will it was an overdose. I never knew my father, and I only know this story because Mom used to tell it to me over and over, the bitterness in her voice palpable. She said he'd OD'd to save on paying alimony.

"I'm sorry."

I wave a hand away, because from what my mother told me, my father didn't deserve anyone's pity.

"I never knew him." The only picture I have of him is one Mom kept of the three of us when I was a few months old. They're looking at each other and smiling like there's a joke they're sharing at the exact moment the picture was taken. I never saw Mom smile like that again.

"My mother passed when I was eleven."

A cool breeze whips down the main street, and I hug my arms in front of my chest. Will notices and pulls me toward him. He too discards his ice cream, and I lean into his warm embrace.

"I'm so sorry, Stella. No child should go through that."

His arms wrap around me and I breathe deep, the confused little girl in me clinging onto a place of safety.

"That must have been so hard on you and Cleo. Did you live with relatives?"

After Mom died, there was no family left, no one to take me. I was sent from foster home to foster home. Slowly, the confused little girl hardened into a mean teenager, running with the wild crowd and breaking the rules of the home. Getting sent from place to place because I was too much trouble, until I came to the Mackeys and met Cleo. I looked up to Cleo. She was the closest thing to a sister I ever had, and she kept me in line. I tried so hard after she left to be good.

But the pull of living on the edge was too strong.

I don't tell Will any of this. We've got one more night together, and I don't want him to think badly of me.

I open my mouth to explain that Cleo isn't my blood sister when there's a shout from across the street.

We turn toward the noise together to see a man collapse to the pavement. He's wearing a leather jacket with a biker's patch indicating he's from the festival. Another man, bald as a bowling ball, stands over him, shaking his shoulders and yelling at him to get up.

"Something's wrong."

I dart across the road, not noticing if Will follows me or not. The man needs medical attention, and I may be able to help.

"What happened?" I crouch next to the biker on the ground and feel his pulse. He's alive, but his breathing is shallow.

"He just collapsed," wails the bald man. His pupils are small pinpricks, and he wavers on his feet.

I lift the biker's arm, and his skin is clammy. When I let go, his arm drops limply to the ground.

"Call an ambulance," I say to Will who's followed me across the street. "He's ODing."

Will gets his phone out and makes the call.

"No ambulances, man." The friend looks panicked. "The police can't get involved."

"Your friend is going to die if we don't get him help."

My training kicks in and I do what I can, rolling him into the recovery position and checking that his airway is clear.

I give him a hard tap on the cheek. "Hey, you need to wake up."

The man gurgles but doesn't respond.

"An ambulance will be here in ten minutes." Will crouches next to the man. "What do you need me to do?"

"If his heart rate drops, we'll need to do CPR."

Will nods. "We need to find out what he's taken." He stands up, but the friend has slunk off. He hasn't gotten far on his unsteady feet, and Will strides up the road to find him.

He catches up with the guy, and I hear raised voices. But I have to concentrate on the man on the ground.

I keep checking his pulse and trying to get him to wake up until the ambulance arrives.

But when it pulls in, I stand up and fade into the background, letting Will give an account of what happened.

I don't want to be associated with a person ODing

either, even if it has nothing to do with me. I can't afford for it to get back to my parole officer.

The paramedics administer Naloxone then load the man into the ambulance. They take off with sirens wailing and I watch with my hand to my chest, hoping the man's going to be okay.

"That was pretty impressive."

I turn at the sound of Will's voice, and the sight of him helps calm my nerves. "I did some volunteer work with a War on Drugs street team."

I leave out the fact that it was part of my community service. Will doesn't need to know about that.

The man's friend comes stumbling back from wherever he was hiding when the ambulance arrived.

"Is he going to be all right?"

Will turns to him, and there's fury in his voice. "What were you thinking, bringing gear to a family festival? There are kids around."

The man holds up his hands, but Will doesn't back down. "It's irresponsible. You want a kid to see that happen?"

"Chill out, bro."

"I'm not your fucking bro. You're lucky I don't know any cops around here, or I'd have them take you in."

The man's face goes red. "You need to relax, smoke a joint or something."

"You need to get the fuck out of my face."

The man backs off, and Will strides up the street. I've never seen him so angry, and I have to jog to keep up with him.

"Are you okay?"

He shakes his head. "If there's one thing I can't tolerate, it's drugs."

He strides off up the street, and this time I let him go. It's lucky this is only for the weekend, because if Will knew about my past, he wouldn't want anything to do with me.

8

WILL

I wake tangled in Stella's limbs, her warm sleepy body crushed against mine. We spent last night together in the motel room while the festival carried on without us.

My appetite for her is insatiable, and I took my fill last night.

Sunlight falls over her cheeks, highlighting her smooth fresh skin. Her hair fans out across the pillow, encasing me in her floral scent.

I could get used to this, waking every morning with Stella next to me. My chest constricts knowing this is our last morning together. In a few hours, I'll be on my bike heading back east, and she'll be heading west.

I should have gone yesterday. I have clients to get back to, but having one more day with Stella overrode any client commitments.

Carefully, I extract my arm from around her and grab my phone from the nightstand.

There are two missed calls and several emails.

I scroll through them, trying to get my head back into work mode. Maxine has done a good job of responding for me. I make a mental note to buy her some of the donuts she likes when I get back.

I'll have to make some client calls today, but as I glance down at the sleepy-eyed woman looking up at me through thick lashes, all thoughts of work flee my mind. I'm not giving up any of my time with Stella to speak to a client.

"Morning, beautiful."

She smiles, and it hits me right in the chest. I put my phone down on the nightstand and draw her to me.

"I've got morning breath," she protests as I nibble on her bottom lip.

"I don't care."

As soon as her lips touch mine, fire ignites in my belly. I've never been turned on so much by a woman as I am by Stella, and a little morning breath isn't going to diminish that.

Her naked body presses against mine, and her nipples scrape against my chest. We slept naked last night, and the thrill of her bare skin against mine makes my dick lengthen.

Even though I took her twice again last night, I still want her with a need I've never felt before. My body craves her.

This will be the last time we're together.

The thought causes a pang in my chest and I kiss her

hard, fighting down the emotions that threaten to swell out of me.

This is only a fling. It can't be anything else. But the poignancy of it being our last time makes me want to enjoy Stella in a way I haven't before.

I run my fingertips over the tiger tattoo on her shoulder. "What's the story behind this?"

The tiger snarls at me like it wants to bite my finger off. It's a badass tattoo and seems out of sync with the thoughtful, caring woman I've come to know.

"Put it down to a wild youth."

I raise an eyebrow at her, and she looks away. There's more to Stella than what I'm seeing, I'm sure of it. I want to know about her misspent youth and every part of her.

But we've only got two more hours together. Sharing the past is not what you do when you're having a weekend fling.

A heaviness settles on my chest. I'll never know the story of the tiger tattoo. I'll never know how she got the tiny scar on her right shoulder. I'll never know about her first boyfriend or what she dreamed she'd be when she was a little girl.

Our short time together doesn't allow for those intimacies.

"What are you thinking about?" She props herself onto her elbow to look at me. The sheet falls off her chest, exposing one perfect breast.

"I was thinking that I wish we didn't live so far away from each other."

She smiles sadly, and our eyes meet. If circumstances

were different, I could get lost in those eyes. I could take her out properly and get to know her, discover what makes her laugh and what makes her sad.

"But we do live far apart," she says wistfully.

There's nothing we can do about it. We'll never know if this could have been something more than a weekend of great sex.

Her finger traces the outline of her breast and I watch, hypnotized, as she twists her nipple in her finger-tips. The nipple hardens under her touch, and she gasps at the sensation.

My cock twitches, and I give in to Stella. I give in to the weekend fling and the great sex. This will be our last time together, and I want it to mean something.

My hands slide under the sheets and over her hips. The skin is smooth and soft, and I love the feel of her under my palms. My body presses against hers, and we kiss long and slow while my hands run over her body.

My lips move to her neck and throat, and I shuffle down the bed to trail kisses over her chest. One hand slides up her back while the other cups her breast as I kiss every part of her soft skin. My tongue flicks her nipples and she arches her back, moaning softly.

I'm going to miss her perfect breasts that have been emblazoned on my brain ever since I walked in on her in the shower. I take my time, committing every detail to memory. The soft pink of the aureola, the texture of her nipple under my tongue, the scent of soap and perspiration and something uniquely Stella.

I move down her body, kissing every part of her soft

belly until I come to her downy mound. My hands run up her thighs, sticky from our nighttime antics. I kiss the tops of her thighs as I trace a slow path to the place between her legs.

Stella parts her thighs, and I move into the space between. She gasps as my mouth closes around her. Her musky scent fills my senses and I commit it to memory along with her taste, wondering if I'll ever taste anything so sweet again.

"Will…" she gasps as my tender kisses reach her most sensitive place. I cast my eyes upward, and Stella is propped up on her elbows watching me. Our eyes lock and I kiss her pussy slowly, giving it the same attention as I have the rest of her glorious body.

My tongue flicks inside, and her eyes roll backwards in pleasure. She cries out, and I commit the sound to memory too. I wish I could bottle this moment up and take it home.

But I can't, and so I keep kissing and licking and sucking slowly and gently until Stella's writhing on the bed moaning my name.

Her hands tangle in my hair, and she moves her hips to ride over my tongue until finally she falls over the edge. Her pussy pulses on my tongue as the climax seizes her body.

I wait for her to come down, then I slide up the bed. She looks at me with dreamy, satisfied eyes, and I could get used to that look.

"That was incredible," Stella gasps.

Her thighs open, and I nestle between them. Our eyes

lock, and I pause. This is the first time we've made love like this, on the bed locked together and facing each other.

It's intimate, and I like it.

With our gaze locked, I slide my tip into her. Stella gasps, and her expression turns needy.

But I want to take my time here too. I kiss her swollen lips and run my hands over her cheek as I push deeper, until she has all of me inside of her.

My body shudders a sigh of relief that it's found its home.

Emotion rumbles inside my chest and I kiss her harder, showing with my body what I can't express in words. What I have no right to express.

I want to tell her that she's smart and funny, and I wish this was more. But what's the point? We both know this is just for the weekend. There's no way we could make it work even if we wanted to.

Instead, I kiss her hard and show her with my body that she's come to mean more to me than a weekend fling.

Her legs wrap around my back and I thrust deeper, watching how every movement lights her up. We rock and sway and take our time. I kiss every part of her I can reach, her throat, her breasts, her neck, and always coming back to her lips.

"Will, I'm going to…"

Her eyes find mine, and they're wild with the force of the orgasm building inside her. Our gazes lock, and she's sexy and vulnerable and beautiful.

Her pussy contracts and she cries out, and watching Stella come undone sends me over the edge.

"Stella…"

I explode into her with a force the makes me cry out her name. I give her everything I've got, my emotions pouring out of me and into her.

The climax lasts for a long time, and when it finishes, I don't want this moment to end. I stay inside her as I roll to the side, pulling her into my arms and planting kisses on the tiger tattoo.

9

STELLA

I bury my head in Will's chest, breathing in his scent and listening to his heartbeat. My own heart races as I come down from the lovemaking session we just had. Because that's what that was: slow, gentle lovemaking.

A final goodbye before we go our separate ways. My heart feels heavy, but even if distance wasn't an issue, there's no way I could be with a straight-laced lawyer like Will.

Everything's black and white for him, and if he found out about my past, he wouldn't want anything to do with me. It's best this is left as a fling, no matter how right it feels to be held in his strong arms.

I must doze off, because I wake with a start as Will moves.

"You want breakfast?" My stomach rumbles at the word and Will looks down, amused. "I take it that's a yes."

"Breakfast sounds good."

"I'll get us a couple of breakfast sandwiches from the place across the road." Will slides out of bed, and a cool shiver runs through me. I sit up and pull the sheets around my chest.

Dull morning light comes through the curtains, and the splatter of rain hits the windows. Not a great day to be riding home.

I watch Will pull on his boxer shorts and riding leathers, a reminder that we'll soon be going our separate ways.

"What time's check out?"

He frowns as he pulls his jacket on. "Ten o'clock. We've got an hour."

It feels like a sentence. An hour to spend together before I never see Will again.

"Stay right here." He leans over the bed and kisses me on the forehead. "I'll be back in five minutes."

I wish I could stay right here. I wish I could stay right here forever.

The door closes behind him, and I climb out of bed. As much as my body craves Will, I want the last love-making session to be how I remember him.

I decide against a shower because I don't want to wash his scent off me. I want to keep a part of Will with me as long as I can.

I grab a fresh t-shirt out of my duffle bag and pull my clothes on. I'm just brushing my hair when there's an urgent knock on the door.

"Stella, are you in there?"

I open the door to find Cleo. Charlie clings to her, and his face is red and his crying pitiful.

"Charlie's sick." She has dark circles under her eyes and probably hasn't slept. "I think it's a respiratory virus again." Charlie's been sick before and spent two nights in the hospital the last time.

"We need to get going. The nearest medical center is an hour away. I've got an emergency appointment. It's on the route home. But we have to leave now."

My stomach knots. I thought I'd have a little more time with Will. But I'm not going to ride back without Cleo and the Crows.

"Right now?"

She shifts Charlie onto her other hip and rubs the top of his head. "Kray's packing the bikes. We'll be ready to roll out in five minutes."

My stomach drops, and she must see the look on my face. "Say your goodbyes, hon," she says gently. "It's time to go."

Charlie lets out a wail and she jiggles him on her hip, whispering words of comfort as she kisses the top of his head.

I can't ask her to stay any longer. Not with a sick child and not after everything she's done for me, taking me in when I needed somewhere to find my feet.

"I'll meet you at the bikes in five."

She's already turned away before I close the door.

My bag's half packed, and I grab the rest of my clothes scattered around the room and retrieve my toiletries from the bathroom.

Will should be back any moment, and there will just be enough time to scarf my breakfast and say goodbye.

But five minutes later my bag is loaded onto my bike, and there's no sign of Will.

I stand on the walkway outside our room and grip the railing tight. The roar of bikes and hum of conversation hangs over the parking lot. Lots of people are leaving today, and the parking lot is full of bikers loading their gear.

I scan the crowds looking for Will, but I don't see him. The breakfast place he went to is across the road and around the corner, and I can't see it from here.

"You ready?" Cleo calls up to me.

I strain my neck, scanning the bodies down below, but I don't see Will.

Charlie lets out a mournful wail, and Cleo holds him to her chest. "We gotta go, Stella."

She's right. I can't wait any longer. Maybe it's for the best. Maybe it's better that there's no goodbye, that the last memory will be of making love this morning.

"One minute," I call down.

I duck back into the hotel room and rummage in my purse until I find a scrap of paper and a pen. I scribble a quick note for Will and leave it on the bedside table.

With one final glance around the motel room, I pull the door shut behind me.

10

WILL

*T*he line for the Breakfast Breaker stretches around the corner. I curse under my breath as I join the line. I'm wasting pressure minutes that I could be with Stella.

I'm still reeling from our session this morning. How perfectly we fit together. How right she felt in my arms.

How I wanted to hold her tight and never let her go.

The thought of leaving her in an hour makes my chest tighten.

I've never met anyone like Stella before. She's thoughtful and funny, and she makes me feel things in a way I never have before.

I've spent the morning wishing we lived closer so we could get to know each other and see if this could work. But as I stand in a line of hungover bikers, the realization hits me.

I don't need to see if this could work. I already know, deep in my bones, that Stella is the only woman for me.

I want to wake up next to her every day. I want to come home to her and make love to her and make her smile every day of my life.

I don't care what it takes. We'll find a way to be together. Maybe she'll want to move to the mountain, or I'll come to her. Whatever it takes, this isn't the end of our story.

My heart feels lighter, and I can't wait to get back to the motel room to see if she feels the same. And if she does, then I'll do whatever it takes. If I have to up and move to the Sunset Coast, I'll do it.

It takes a good ten minutes to get to the front of the line, but I'm not coming back empty-handed. I order two double bacon sandwiches and a large coffee just how she likes it.

I'm humming to myself as I grab my order. I can't wait to tell her how I feel and figure out how the hell we're going to make this work. I'm sure she feels the same. There's no denying the connection between us.

My phone buzzes in my pocket, and I stop at a bench to put my coffees down and take the call.

It's Maxine, and she's got a client desperate to talk to me. His deposition hearing is next week, and he's freaking out about it.

I take the call and spend ten minutes reassuring him and going over our approach. Finally, the man's calm and I'm able to hang up.

It's been over twenty minutes since I left Stella, and I wonder if she's still waiting for me in bed, warm and soft.

The parking lot is busy as guests pack up their bikes and hit the road. I take the stairs to the walkway two at a time and push open the door to the hotel room.

The bed's empty and the covers have been hastily pulled up.

"Stella?"

Her bag is gone, and the room seems empty without her clothes strewn everywhere. She must be loading up the bikes with Cleo.

I put the food and coffee down on the table, and my fingers brush a piece of paper with writing scrawled across.

My gaze darts over the writing.

Will,

   Thank you for the most amazing fling ever.
   I'll never forget you.
   Stella xx

It feels like someone's punched me in the stomach. The air expels from my lungs, and I can't breathe. I grab the note and read it again, not believing what I read.

She can't be gone. It can't end like this.

I race out of the motel room and along the walkway to Cleo's room. A cleaning cart is parked outside, and the door is half open.

I push into the room and a woman in an apron looks up at me, startled.

"The people that were staying in this room, where are they?"

She shrugs. "They're gone. Checked out ten minutes ago.

Ten minutes isn't long when you've got kids and bags to organize. They might still be in the parking lot.

I race out of the room and down the stairs, bumping into a man as I go.

"Watch it!" he calls after me.

The parking lot's full of people loading their bikes up. I head to the corner where the Underground Crows were parked.

But there's no sign of Stella or any of them or the van that Cleo was driving with the kids.

I dart around the parking lot looking for Stella or Cleo or anyone they were with. But when ten o'clock rolls around and Luke finds me in a near empty parking lot, I have to face the truth.

It might have meant more to me, but to Stella it was just a fling.

I realized too late I have feelings for her, and now, Stella is gone.

Six months later…

*R*ain splatters the windows of the Wild Taste Bar and Restaurant, making it difficult to concentrate on the report in front of me.

I've taken to working in a corner table at HQ some days just in case Stella turns up looking for me.

"Give me five minutes and I could put you out of your misery."

Bit Rate slides into the seat next to me and opens his laptop. He pulls on his beard thoughtfully. "Might take a bit longer if we need to use facial recognition."

It's not the first time he's offered to hack into systems to try to find Stella.

I fix him with a wary look. "Is it legal?"

Bit Rate scratches his beard and looks away. "It's the quickest way to find her."

Which tells me everything I need to know. As tempting as what he's offering is, I can't be on the wrong side of the law.

Which leaves me at the mercy of Cleo, waiting until she hears from Stella.

It took me a few weeks of wallowing in self-pity to realize I wasn't going to forget Stella easily. And to realize that maybe what she wrote on the note wasn't all she was feeling.

When I replay the weekend in my mind there's definitely a connection between us, and she must have felt it too. The way she nestled into me, the way our bodies gravitated to each other overnight, the last time we made love.

If only I'd said something to her then, maybe things might have been different. But I told her it was a fling from the start, and I never said it was anything else. Of course she wasn't going to wait around for a guy who only wanted a fling. I guess when the Crows left, she went with them.

By the time I got myself off my own ass and tried to track her down, she was gone.

I took a trip out to the west coast, driving for two days straight. I went straight to the Underground Crows HQ. Turns out they aren't bad guys after all. Quite hospitable and with as many kids running around their club as we have.

Cleo and Kray were welcoming, but I missed Stella by a few days.

It turns out her and Cleo aren't real sisters, not blood ones anyway. I don't know why Stella didn't tell me. They met when they shared the same foster home for two years.

When I met Stella, she'd been staying with Cleo for two months. And it didn't seem odd to Cleo when she moved on.

Cleo said she often goes long spells without hearing from Stella.

It made me wonder what else I don't know about her. It seemed like there was more Cleo wanted to say but she didn't.

I scoured the coast looking for her. I contacted every long-term care facility on the west coast. But none of them knew of a Stella.

I came back to the mountain frustrated but more determined than ever to find her.

As weeks turned into months, I began to wonder if I imagined that weekend together. If the connection we shared was real.

A hand comes down heavy on my shoulder, and I glance up into the concerned eyes of Bit Rate.

"Maybe it's time to move on, bro. I know it isn't easy. But you look like shit, and your grumpy face is scaring away the customers."

He of all people should know. Bit Rate lost his wife four years ago. It's what propelled him out of the military in a fit of grief and anger.

He went from working intel for the military to raising two small kids on his own. A string of unsuitable nannies means they're often here at the clubhouse and getting in everyone's way. Two wild little girls with a grumpy dad who just wants to hide away at home and lose himself in shoot em' up video games.

He's in here now because there's a problem with the club's internet provider.

Bit Rate manages the IT for the club and its businesses. It's a gross underuse of his skills, but it keeps him close to home where his girls need him.

Maybe he's right and it's time to move on. But whenever I think about giving up on Stella, I remember her easy laugh and soft look and I can't let myself forget her.

"Maybe," I say noncommittally.

STELLA

*T*he shuffle of feet on linoleum has me looking up from the night desk. You never know when one of the residents is going to go for a late-night wander. But it's only Terry, wheeling the cleaning cart out of the ward.

"Night night Stella." He lifts a hand, and I wave in response.

"Night Terry. Drive safe."

He uses his card to buzz through the doors, and they slide back into place behind him.

I hear him opening the cleaning closet and the squeaky wheels of the cart as it rolls away for the night. Then he's gone out the main doors and into the night.

Silence settles over the nursing home, broken by the occasional heavy snore from one of the residents.

The other night warden is on his late break, and I'll wait for him to come back before I do a walk around.

I grab my phone and pull up a picture I took of me

and Will from the first day of the festival. We're smiling, and he's got the bruise on his face. I wonder how it healed and if he's got a scar.

The phone screen goes dead, and I rummage in my purse for my charger. I come up empty handed. I must have left it at home.

I stuff my useless phone in my purse and sigh.

The night shift pays more, and it also gives me time to think. And I've been doing a lot of thinking in the last six months.

The first few days after I left Will, it felt like my heart was bruised. I never knew one person could affect me so much.

Charlie had a respiratory virus, and while he wasn't hospitalized, he was ill for two weeks. It kept me busy at Cleo's helping with Nina and around the house so she could take care of Charlie.

Then she got a call from the agency asking if she could take a kid in who needed an emergency bed. With me taking up the spare room, she had to refuse. It pains Cleo to refuse any of the foster kids who she's asked to care for.

It was time for me to move on.

It was only after I left Cleo's place that I found out what Will had left me growing inside my belly.

It was too late to go back, and I didn't want Cleo to think ill of me. I've been one fuck up after another since our foster care days, and an unwanted pregnancy was just another cliche of foster kid behavior.

Not that it was unwanted. There's comfort in

knowing I'll always have a part of Will with me, even if he can never know.

My parole expired that week also, so I left the west coast and headed inland looking for work.

It was difficult to find someone who would give me a chance, but I finally found work in a nursing home on the outskirts of Salt Lake City.

I found a cheap apartment to rent, and for a while it was enough.

But as the months have gone by and my body changes, swelling with the baby inside me, it terrifies me to think of doing this on my own.

Cleo has reached out to me several times, but I don't take her calls. I let her know I'm okay, and that's it. If she knew my situation, she'd only worry about me, and Cleo has enough people to worry about.

She told me Will turned up at the Underground Crows HQ looking for me. That he rode all the way from North Carolina, practically from coast to coast.

When she told me that my heart soared, only to crash down a second later. I can't burden Will with a child. Not with my past. It could end his career.

There's something about the quiet of the air tonight that makes my heart feel especially sore. Loneliness creeps up on you, and tonight it's overwhelming.

I long to speak to Cleo, to hear her voice and hear how the kids are doing.

I reach for my phone before remembcring the battery's dead. Instead, I pick up the work phone and dial Cleo's number.

She answers briskly. Charlie cries in the background, and there's the sound of a television playing music from a kids' cartoon.

"It's Stella."

"Stella!" Cleo's relief is palpable, and it brings tears to my eyes. There's someone in the world who cares about me. "Where are you?"

I'm not ready to tell her that. Not till after I have the baby. If I tell her now, she'll insist I come back, and the last thing she needs is someone else to worry about.

"I'm fine," I say, pretending to mishear her. "How are the kids?"

She sighs. "They're fine. Good. We've got another boy staying with us. Just arrived last night. But he's settling in well, and Nina's great with him."

I listen to her chatter about her family and bite my cheek to stop from crying. Despite how tired she sounds, she also sounds happy. Cleo was made to be a mom, and the fact that she's taking in foster kids too makes my heart swell. She always did have her head screwed on. Much more than me.

"Have you been in touch with Will? That man's crazy about you."

My heart skips a beat. "Why? What did he say?"

"It's not what he said. It's what he does. He calls me every week, Stella, to ask about you. The man's crazy for you. If you're not interested, then fine. But tell him. Put the poor guy out of his misery. He's driving me nuts."

She's right. I should harden up and message Will. Cleo sent me his number, and I saved it in my phone. She asked if I could give him my number, but I said no. I thought the guy would get the hint that I didn't want to see him. But he's persistent.

"He's a good guy. If you insist on running somewhere, why not run to him?"

Because if he knew what I really was, he'd want nothing to do with me. Because I'm not worthy of him, but I'm too scared to tell him, because if I allow myself to speak to him again, to make contact, I don't think I'd be strong enough to walk away a second time.

"Maybe." I nibble on the end of my fingernail.

There's a shout in the background and muffled voices. "I gotta go. The new kid just hit Nina, and I need to sort this out. Poor thing, he's only five and doesn't understand what's happening. He's scared and lashing out."

"Of course."

"Call me again, please."

She hangs up, and I sink back into silence. The baby kicks, and I run my hand over my belly. In a few months, I'm going to have a child of my own. And I wonder if I can be even half the mother Cleo is.

13
STELLA

A few days later I'm back at work, standing in front of my boss as she tries not to glance at my protruding belly.

"I'm sorry, Stella, but your contract won't be extended after next week."

I was expecting this. No one wants the liability of a heavily pregnant woman working for them.

In a job like this, you need to be physically able to carry out tasks like rolling someone over in bed, helping them to the toilet, and giving them a wash down if they're unable to clean themselves. It's why I was good at it. With my large frame, care work suits me.

Jillian has the decency to look sorry for me. But I don't need her pity. I need a job.

"I'll give you a good reference." She pulls something out of her pocket. "And here's a bonus."

She holds out a hundred dollar bill and thrusts it into my hand. "Something for you and the little one."

The gesture is unexpected, and I sink into the chair. "Thank you."

Tears threaten my eyes, and I blink them away quickly. My hormones are all over the place, and anything makes me well up these days.

"We'll make next Friday your last shift."

"Of course."

Jillian walks away, and I'm left in the quiet of the nurses' station. I lift up my t-shirt and unzip the fanny pack I've taken to wearing and stuff the hundred dollar bill inside. I push down the other bills, mentally counting them in my head and hoping it will be enough for when the baby comes.

The door swishes open and I look up, expecting Terry here for his cleaning shift.

My heart catches in my throat as Will strides through the doors.

His hair is ruffled and stubble lines his chin. He's in his riding leathers and looks like he just slid off the bike.

Our eyes lock, and my breath hitches. He's as breath-taking as I remember—maybe more so seeing him in the flesh.

"I found you." He crosses to the desk. "I've looked all over for you, Stella. I went to see Cleo, but I just missed you, and then she didn't know where you were..."

He breaks off and runs his hand through his hair.

"How did you find me?"

"Cleo gave me the number you called her on last week. Don't be mad at her. I think she wanted some peace; I've been pestering her to give me any news of you. And now I've finally found you."

I've wanted to see Will for so long, to hear his voice, and now that he's in front of me I'm in shock.

I stand up slowly and his eyes run down my body, lingering on my swollen breasts until they land on my belly.

His eyes widen with shock. "You're pregnant?"

14

WILL

*S*tella stuffs chicken wings in her mouth as if she hasn't had a decent meal in weeks. And maybe she hasn't. Her face looks thinner than when we met six months ago, and despite the round belly, it seems like she's lost weight.

The baby bump protrudes in a perfect oval lump. I've been around enough pregnant women at the club to know she's quite far along, about six months along.

Which is just about when our weekend fling took place.

Stella's just finished her shift, and we're sitting at a local diner. I watch her stuff chicken wings in her mouth as questions whir through my brain.

But the first one I have to ask: "Is it mine?"

She chews slowly then swallows. I hold my breath waiting for her answer, conflicting emotions running through my chest.

"Yes."

I let out a long slow breath. I'm going to be a father. The knowledge is a jolt to my heart but not an unpleasant one.

"I thought you were on the pill."

Stella looks down and pushes a thick potato chip around her plate. "I'm not the most reliable person, Will. I must have forgotten to take it. Then it was hectic with Charlie being sick, and by the time I remembered a few days later, I didn't want to take it in case there was already a baby and it did some harm."

She looks defensive, but I'm not going to judge her. Even though the thought of being a father scares the shit out of me, it's also exciting.

"Why did you leave Cleo's? Why did you run away?"

"I didn't run away, Will. This is what I do. I move around places; I was only at Cleo's for a few months. It was time to move on."

She says it defiantly with a brittle note to her voice. Like a woman who's not used to having people around who she wants to stay for.

"But Cleo's family. Does she even know?" I indicate her belly.

"Cleo's not my real family, Will. We were in the same foster home for a few years. We're not real family."

Her voice is small, and my heart aches for this woman. Loneliness reeks out of her and I long to take her in my arms, to show her there are people who care for her if only she'll let them.

"Family is who you choose, Stella. Cleo wouldn't want you to go through this on your own."

Her bottom lip wobbles, and she swipes at her eyes. "I've always been on my own, Will. I can do this on my own too."

She sticks out her chin and looks defiant, daring me to challenge her. Stella's got some idea in her head that she needs to be independent. Well, that stops right now.

I reach across the table and clasp her hands in mine. "You're not on your own anymore, Stella. I've found you, and I'm not going anywhere."

Her eyes narrow, distrustful, but I carry on before she can protest. "I've searched for you for six months. If you don't want to be with me, then I'll respect that. But spend the day with me first. Let me show you we're meant to be together."

She lowers her gaze, and her voice is quiet. "It was supposed to be a fling."

I squeeze her hands. "Come on. Let's go for a ride."

She sighs heavily. "Okay. But I need to pop home to shower and change out of my scrubs."

If she thinks I'm letting her go off on her own, she's crazy. "You're not going to run?"

"No. I'll give you my address. You can meet me there in an hour."

She tells me the address, and we leave the diner. Stella gets on her bike, and I follow at a safe distance. I'm not risking her running from me again. Not after I've finally found her, and especially now that she's carrying my child.

She pulls up outside a small block of apartments. There's graffiti on the wall and paint chips off the window frames. A rusty gate swings on its hinges surrounded by a lawn that hasn't seen a mower in a long while.

My heart aches thinking about Stella staying here. She goes into an apartment on the second floor, and I wait across the road.

An hour later she comes out, and I pretend I just pulled up.

15

STELLA

*W*ind whips my hair as the road speeds underneath me. In front, Will takes a turn to the left following a sign to a local lake.

It's been a long time since I went for a ride just for fun, and it feels good to be on the open road again. As we speed away from the city, I feel lighter. It was a shock to see Will and also a relief.

I've missed him, and I thought I was doing the right thing by not contacting him. But now that he's here, I'm not so sure.

Instead of recoiling at the prospect of being a father, he seems at least curious about it. But could we be a happy family? It seems too good to be true.

We come to the lake and park the bikes in the parking lot.

There's a boardwalk that skirts the lake, and we set off along it. Tall reeds are on either side, and nesting birds call to each other and scurry away as we come near.

A family of swans glides past, the mother at the front followed by three cygnets, and the daddy swan bringing up the rear.

Will takes my hand, and for a while we don't talk about the situation. I ask about his work and the mountain, and I tell him about my job at the nursing home.

It's not until we've circled the lake and are back near the little parking lot that he goes quiet. There's a park bench overlooking the lake, and we take a seat.

Will wipes his hands on his jeans and takes a long breath, suddenly nervous. I wonder what he's going to say, and I brace myself.

This is where he tells me he's going back to the mountain and leaving me to be a single mom. That he's not ready for a kid and he hopes I understand, but it's for the best. He'll probably send money, because he's a guy that does the right thing.

I clutch my arms to my chest, bracing myself for the blow even though I know it's for the best.

But he doesn't say that. Instead, Will takes a small box out of his pocket and sinks to his knees.

"Stella…"

I gasp when I realize what he's doing, the shock of it making my mouth drop open.

"I've searched all over for you, and I can't believe I finally found you. I don't run away from my responsibilities, and I will care for you and the baby as best I can. Will you marry me?"

He opens the box, and a diamond ring sparkles in the

sun. It's a simple gold band with a cluster of small diamonds at the center. It's beautiful.

I reach for the ring, then hesitate.

He must have run out and bought this while I was getting changed. He doesn't want me for me. He just wants to do the right thing.

"You don't have to marry me because I'm knocked up."

Will frowns. "It's not like that."

"I know this isn't what you expected to find, and it's good of you to offer. But I don't want to marry someone just because they're doing the right thing, Will. I'd rather do this on my own from the start than have a man who decides to leave in a few years because he can't handle a baby and a woman he doesn't love."

"Is that what you think?"

He looks hurt, and a pang of doubt hits my stomach. "Isn't it?"

Will shifts on his knee but doesn't get up. "Stella, I've thought about nothing but you since the day you left me in Grantstown. I drove across the country and spent a week hanging out with the damned Underground Crows hoping you'd come back, hoping you'd send word to Cleo about where you are. I've bothered her every week since you left, and when she told me the name of the facility you called her from, I came straight to you.

"I love you Stella, I want to be with you. I want to take you back to Wild Heart Mountain with me to show you what family looks like.

"I bought this ring the week I drove to the coast to

find you. I've been wanting to marry you since the morning we made love in the hotel, and I finally realized this was more than a fling. It's love. It's a big love. I'm empty without you, Stella. I'm lost.

"We're two orphans, and we can start our own family. Sure, this baby is a little ahead of schedule, but that doesn't matter. I love you, Stella."

Tears sting my eyes at his words. It's more than I ever dreamed of. The love of a good man and the chance to be a family.

"So I'm going to ask you again. Will you marry me?"

I look into his eyes and see nothing but love. There's still so much Will doesn't know about me.

He may not want to marry me when he learns the truth. I should tell him right now. But months of loneliness and longing makes my heart ache.

I want him. I've denied it for so long. I'll tell him tomorrow, and I have to believe that he'll understand. But right now, I just want to follow my heart and believe everything will be all right.

"Yes. Yes, I will."

He slides the ring on my finger, and it glints in the afternoon sun.

Will gets off his knees and pulls me into a hug. He's laughing, and I'm crying tears of happiness. He kisses me hard, and it feels so good to have his arms around me again.

But there's a niggle in my gut about what will happen when he learns the truth.

16

WILL

*W*e ride straight to my hotel room. Tomorrow I'll arrange to pack up Stella's belongings and get them sent here. She told me she has a week left on her contract, and I call Maxine to tell her I'll be working remotely for a week. My clients will have to wait.

I'm not leaving Stella's side until I have her safely back at Wild Heart Mountain. I'll arrange to get the bikes shipped back, and I'll hire a car to drive us and her stuff back. I don't want her riding all those miles in her condition.

We park the bikes outside the motel, and I take her hand to lead her to my room. I can't believe I've finally got Stella beside me, and I grasp her hand firmly. The ring presses into my flesh, and the warmth of her skin sends heat skittering through my body.

Even before we get to my room, I'm hard for her.

I've spent six months fantasizing about Stella, and

now that she's in my room I can't wait any longer. As soon as we shut the door behind us, I pull her close.

Her baby mound bumps against me and I run my hands over it, enjoying the new shape of her body.

"I missed you." I breathe in her scent as I nuzzle my face into her neck.

"I missed you too." It comes out as a sigh, and she sags against me. I hold her cheeks in my palms and notice the dark circles under her eyes and the creases that weren't there before.

She's been carrying this load all by herself, and now I'm here to unburden her.

I kiss her cheeks and her lips and trail my mouth down her neck. Stella gives a little sigh of pleasure that I feel all the way in my dick.

"Come here." I lead her over to the bed and she sits on the edge, her legs parted to accommodate her baby bump.

I kneel before her and nestle between her thighs. I'm not sure what the protocol is when you're pregnant. I want her like crazy but don't want to cause her discomfort.

"Are you okay to make love?"

She smiles shyly up at me. "I don't know. I haven't tried it."

Relief floods me at those words. I haven't been with anyone either and I hoped she hadn't, but it's good to hear the confirmation.

"Tell me if anything feels uncomfortable."

She traces her fingers down my arms, and the hairs stand to attention. "I will."

Her touch fires my desire, and I slide my hands around her waist and draw her into me. Our lips collide, and six months of longing pours into the kiss.

My body aches for Stella and so does my heart. To hold her in my arms again touches a place deep inside of me. Since I lost my parents and then my sister, I've been lost. But with Stella, I'm home again.

My hands slide under her jacket, and I slip it off her shoulders. Her arms pimple with the sudden cold and I run my hands over her skin, warming her up. She's wearing a t-shirt that strains against her chest, and I slide it over her head and feast my eyes on her perfect swollen breasts.

They're larger than when I first met her and just as perfect.

I cup them in my palm and run a finger over her nipple. Stella sucks in her teeth and jerks back.

"They're a little sensitive right now."

I pull away from her breasts and move my hand down to her waist. I've been dreaming about her breasts, but I'll have to wait another few months to play out my fantasies.

Stella reaches forward and hooks her thumb under my t-shirt and pulls it off my head. Her fingers trace over my skin, and I suck in a breath at the sensation.

She reaches my belt and undoes it in a flurry of need. We pull at each other's clothes, discarding them in a pile on the floor.

I roll with her onto the bed, the baby bump not stopping me from entwining my body with hers.

"It might help if I go on top." Stella rolls on top of me, and I lie back as she climbs over me.

The sight before me is a vision. Stella rising above me, her baby bump and swollen breasts lending new curves to her voluptuous body.

"I've missed this so much," she moans as she slides me between her folds.

I let Stella guide me, and her gaze finds mine as she sinks onto me. I groan in pleasure as she engulfs me in her sticky heat.

My hands find her hips, needing to hold onto her, and I grind her down on me until I fill every inch of her.

It's better than I remembered, it's better than I've fantasized about. It feels like coming home.

"Stella…" This is better than anything I could have imagined, and I can't find the words to tell her how much she means to me.

Stella leans forward, and her hair trails down my chest.

"I love you," I whisper.

"I love you too."

Her hands clasp the headboard and she grinds into me, moving her hips in a hypnotic sway. I watch my woman bring herself to climax, and when she comes down I take her hips and lift her up and down my shaft until I too fall into oblivion. To a place where nothing else matters but the feel of her wrapped around me.

Afterwards we lie in each other's arms, talking about everything we've been doing during our time apart.

I order takeout and we lie in bed eating straight out of the cartons.

Stella rubs her belly and swings her legs out of bed. "I need to stretch my legs."

She pulls on a robe and paces the room with one hand protectively on her baby bump. "It gets uncomfortable sitting in one place for too long."

"You want to go for a walk?" It's nearly midnight, but if she wants to walk then that's what we'll do.

"The baby's always active at night."

We pull on our clothes and head out into the night. I keep my arm around Stella and we walk a few blocks, talking about our plans for moving to the mountain.

I tell her about the MC and the other old ladies and how they'll be able to give advice and help when the baby comes.

"There's a medical center in Hope that might have work, but you don't need to work if you don't want to. If you want to stay home and raise our kids, that's fine too."

"Kids?" Her eyebrows raise into the air.

I place a hand on her belly and feel the life growing in there. "We're not stopping at one. I want a large family. We're starting our own empire here. Let's make it a big one."

Stella smiles a tight smile and doesn't say anything. She stops walking and turns to me. We're next to a small park, and her face is half in shadow from a large tree that we've stopped under.

"I need to tell you something."

My heart sinks. She's changed her mind; she doesn't want to come back with me. She really does want to raise the baby on her own.

"What is it?"

She opens her mouth to speak when a movement from the park catches my eye. I pull her toward me and put my finger to my lips to silence her.

A man walks down the pathway in the center of the park. His steps are quick, his hands are in his pockets, and he glances furtively around him from under a hoody. The tree shields us from view, and I pull Stella further into the shadows.

As the man in the hoody reaches the end of the path, another man steps out of the shadows. They nod to each other, and without speaking the man in the hoody sticks his hand out. They shake hands, exchanging something. The man steps back and blends into the shadows, while the hoody man jogs out of the park.

I pull Stella away from the park and back towards the hotel. I've got my phone out, and I note the name of the street as I put in a call to the police.

"Drug dealer," I mouth to Stella. "Get inside the motel and don't come out until I knock."

She looks like she wants to say something, but she doesn't argue.

Once she's safely inside, I call the local police and tell them what I saw. I tell them exactly where they can find the dealer. They promise to send someone, and I hope they get the fucker.

When I get back to the hotel, Stella's on the bed rubbing her belly thoughtfully.

"I hope they get that scum," I mutter.

She nibbles on her nails. "Why are you so tough on drugs?"

I pace the room, the anger raging inside me. "Because they destroy lives."

She looks upset, and I sit on the bed and take a deep breath to calm the rage. "Sorry, I'm not angry at you. I lost my sister to a drug overdose."

Her face floods with sympathy, and she takes my hands. "I'm so sorry."

There are tears in her eyes and that means something to me, that she feels my pain.

"After our parents passed, I went into the military. Cara was away at college, and I thought she was okay. She was my older sister and always seemed to have it together."

I run a hand over my face at the painful memory. Cara was bubbly and outgoing. I didn't understand until it was too late that her attitude hid an internal struggle.

"Her roommate told me that it started with smoking pot at frat parties. But after my parents died, she got into harder stuff. She was prescribed anti-depressants, and when they stopped her prescription, she found other ways to procure what she needed to numb the pain.

"Her roommate found her one night passed out and couldn't revive her. The ambulance was called, but she was already gone. She had a combination of alcohol and Fentanyl in her system."

I take a deep breath as the memory of that call floods my brain. I was posted in Afghanistan and didn't hear about Cara until two days after she died. I came straight home, not believing that my bright sister could go out like that.

"The police found a stash in her room. Someone sold a vulnerable woman that shit, and I will never forgive them for it. Drug dealers are the scum of the earth. They should all be locked up with no chance of parole."

My fist slams into my palm, and Stella jumps. She's got her knees pulled up to her chest, and she's gone pale.

I'm an idiot for getting angry and scaring her. I run my hands down her arms. She's cold, and I need to get her into bed. "Are you okay?"

Stella bites the end of her fingernail, and when she looks at me there are tears in her eyes. "I'm so sorry about your sister."

She's whispering and pale, and I'm suddenly aware it's almost 1:00 a.m. and she's pregnant, and I should be looking after her and not bringing up things that happened in the past that I can't change.

"Let's get some sleep."

Stella doesn't say a word as she changes into her pajamas and uses the bathroom. By the time I'm finished brushing my teeth, she's lying on her side. I snuggle into her, annoyed at myself for keeping her up late.

I have to take better care of my future wife.

The next morning Stella is quiet, and I kick myself for keeping her up. She's back on night shift tonight, and that means she can stay in bed all day as far as I'm concerned.

I leave her under the blanket while I go to take a shower.

While I wait for the shower to heat up, my phone buzzes. It's Bit Rate.

"There's something you need to see."

My skin prickles at his serious tone. "What is it?"

"Don't shoot the messenger, but I did some digging on your girl."

I let out a slow breath. "You don't need to do that. I found her."

"I know. That's the problem." There's the high-pitched squeal of one of his girls in the background, and he shouts at them to be quiet. "Damned kids. Don't have em, Judge."

Too late, I almost say. "How did you know I found her?"

"I saw Maxine. She was having trouble with her laptop."

It surprises me how quickly gossip spreads on the side of a mountain.

"Did she speak to you about her niece?" Maxine's niece is returning soon from being an au pair in France, and I mentioned her to Bit Rate. She'd be perfect to look after his girls.

"I don't need another damned nanny. Not after the last one. Me and the girls are fine. It's not me you need to worry about. I did a little digging on your soon to be wife."

"Bit Rate," I growl, because I don't like where this is heading. "Is it legal?"

"Kinda. I found some interesting things in the almost public record."

I shake my head. "Not interested. Whatever digging you did could get me fired. I know everything I need to know about Stella." Even as I say it, I know it's not true. I don't know about her past. She doesn't talk about it, and I haven't pressed because it seems painful to her.

"You don't know about this." His tone gives me pause. What do I really know about my fiancé?

"Maybe you already know and you're all good with it, but if you don't, then you need to know. I'll email it over, and you decide if you want to look at it or not."

"Don't do that." The last thing I need is a trail of illegal hacking pointing straight to me.

"Already done it."

I sigh heavily. Just because he's sent it doesn't mean I have to look at it.

I end the call and step into the shower. Hot water cascades over me, making my skin tingle with the heat.

I won't look at the email. I'll delete it and let Stella tell me anything she needs to tell me in her own time.

But Bit Rate wouldn't send it to me if he wasn't concerned.

Still, it's none of my business. Whatever Stella did in the past is in the past.

My thoughts ping pong back and forth, and I stay in the shower until the water runs cold wondering what to do.

By the time I get out of the bathroom, I've decided to speak to Stella first. To give her the opportunity to tell me if there's something she needs to tell me. I step out of the bathroom with a towel wrapped around me.

Stella's not in bed where I left her.

"Stella..."

I spin around the room slowly. Her clothes are gone, her purse is gone. There's no sign of Stella.

She's run away again.

I knew something was off with her this morning when she was so quiet. I shouldn't have left her on her own.

I sink onto the bed and pull up my email app. The message from Bit Rate is at the top. With trembling fingers, I hit open.

It's a report from the California corrections department. A criminal register for Stella Lipton. My blood goes cold. Stella's got a criminal record.

I scan the email, and my fists clench when I get to the felony.

Possession of drugs with intent to distribute.

The air explodes out of my lungs, and I can't breathe.

Stella's a convicted drug dealer.

18
STELLA

I hold the breakfast sandwiches in one hand as I dig in my pocket for the room key. After a restless night thinking about Will's sister, I can't put it off any longer. I have to come clean to Will. If he doesn't want to be with me after I tell him about my past, then I understand, but he deserves to know the truth.

My heart's hammering in my chest as I push open the door.

"I got us breakfast." I hold up the paper bags. It's a small peace offering before I tell him. Besides, my baby wouldn't let me go another minute without breakfast.

Will's sitting on the bed wrapped in a towel and holding his phone. His face is pale, and when he looks up his mouth is set in a grim line. It's as if I'm looking at a stranger.

He knows.

The air goes out of my lungs, and I drop the paper bags on the floor.

"Will…?" My voice is barely a whisper.

"When were you going to tell me, Stella?" His tone is icy and I shiver, wrapping my arms around myself.

"I was going to tell you now. I came back to explain."

He stands up and his muscles ripple across his bare torso, but this is no time to appreciate his cut abs.

"I'm listening."

His voice is clipped, and this must be his professional tone, the straight-laced attorney who's always on the right side of the law.

"I went wild after my mom died." I hate blaming her for this, but my therapist taught me to own the trauma, to recognize the impact it had on me. "I went from foster home to foster home, passed around like a thing nobody wanted."

His expression softens slightly, and there's empathy in his look. "It doesn't excuse any of the things that I did." I take a deep breath. My therapist also taught me to own my actions and to be accountable for the choices I made, even the bad ones.

"Cleo kept me straight for a while, but when she aged out of the system, I went off the rails for a few years."

He folds his arms across his chest, and I keep talking.

"I got in with a bad crowd. I didn't fully understand what they were doing. We used to hang out at a local basketball court, and lots of people would stop by. I never knew they were selling drugs."

He raises his eyebrows at me and I know how that sounds, but it's true. Kind of. I knew in the back of my mind that something was going down, but it was never talked about and I never asked questions. As I grew older, I began to realize I didn't want to be there. I didn't want to hang around these so-called friends anymore. But they were all I had.

"One night I had been drinking."

"Just drinking?" There's accusation in his voice, but I don't blame him for asking.

"Yes. Just drinking. The police turned up, and we ran. Someone threw a backpack to the ground, and I stumbled over it and tripped. The police caught me with the backpack full of drugs and cash."

The memory still makes me bitter, that the worst offenders got away and I was the one caught red-handed. I didn't even know what was in the backpack. But the police didn't believe me. In their eyes, I was one more problem they were getting off the street.

I had just turned eighteen and got the full force of the law.

"I went to prison." I say it quietly, ashamed to admit it to this man who's done nothing but good with his life. "It was the low point of a pretty shit life."

Will uncrosses his arms and takes half a step towards me. Then stops. There's indecision on his face, and I can't blame him for that.

"I got therapy for the first time. I worked through the trauma of losing my mom and saw how destructive my behavior had been since. I vowed to do better. I promised myself I'd change."

"Is this why you ran?"

I nod. "I'm one fuck-up after another, Will. I knew if

you knew the truth about me, you wouldn't want anything to do with me. You're a lawyer. You can't be with someone with a criminal record. And when I found out about your sister…"

I slide the ring off my finger. "I can't ask you to forgive me for what I've done. I have to live with the consequences of my actions every day of my life."

I put the ring on the table by the door, and when I look at Will, his eyes are shiny with tears.

"I'm sorry you wasted a trip out here."

He doesn't say anything, but he doesn't try to stop me either. I'm fighting tears as I open the motel door room and step outside.

He doesn't follow me as I cross the parking lot and get on my bike.

As I ride back to my apartment, I let the tears flow. But I feel lighter. At least he knows what I am. I've told him the entire truth about me. At least that's one less burden to carry.

WILL

*T*he motel door clicks shut behind Stella, and I listen to her footsteps as she walks away. Part of me longs to follow her, but the other part of me is so angry at her for not telling me sooner.

Conflicting emotions fight for space in my heart. I feel for the adolescent Stella, passed from foster home to foster home, scared and heartbroken, wanting somewhere to belong.

It took all of my restraint not to go to her and fold her into my arms.

But I can't overlook what she did. She dealt drugs. She sold drugs to people just like Cara. She could be responsible for the deaths of users. Users with families left heartbroken by their losses.

Since Cara's overdose, I've been hard on my stance on drugs. There's no place for them in this world, and dealers are scum. But Stella's situation sounds like she's a victim as well. A victim of a shitty system that left her broken and scared and with not many choices.

And if what she says is true, she wasn't doing the dealing, just hanging around with a bad crowd and in the wrong place at the wrong time.

I run a hand through my wet hair and pull on the ends.

"Fuck."

For the last ten years, since Cara died, I've campaigned for harsher penalties on drug dealers. I've donated to causes and given free legal aid for families who have lost someone to drugs.

How can I give my heart to someone who sits on the other side of that?

My clothes are on the floor where I left them last night, and I pull them on with a heavy heart. The bedsheets are crumpled, and I think back to our lovemaking last night. Only twelve hours ago I was the happiest man in the world. I had found Stella, and I finally felt anchored. Ready to bring her home and start our family.

Now I'm a man on his own again, on his one-man crusade against drugs.

I pull on my leather jacket and pick up the ring from the table.

No wonder she ran from Cleo's. She knew I wouldn't want to be with her when I learned the truth. And stupid fool that I am, I found her anyway.

I turn the ring over in my fingers. I can't imagine the Stella I know doing all those things she told me about.

If she was a troubled youth off the rails, then she's changed her life around. She works in a nursing home looking after vulnerable people. She volunteered for the War on Drugs street team.

People can change. She's proven it.

Maybe some people do deserve a second chance. Maybe the answer isn't tougher penalties but rehabilitation and education.

Stella made bad choices, and she's paid for them. Does she need to keep paying for the rest of her life?

I take a steady breath as the emotions that have been fighting inside me settle into place.

There's no excusing what Stella did. But there's no denying my feelings for her. I love Stella, and I'm not giving up on her.

If she can change, I can change.

I grab my helmet and head for the door. I just hope I'm not too late to catch her this time.

20
STELLA

$\mathcal{I}$ count out the money from my fanny pack one more time. There's enough to pay rent for one more month, but I don't know what I'll do after that.

I swipe at tears.

I'll have to go back to Cleo's. Will doesn't want me, and I don't blame him. I don't want to be a burden to Cleo, but maybe I can work at the club.

I'll find a way. I always do.

The roar of a bike has me wiping my eyes and running to the window. My heart jumps in my throat when I see Will.

But he's probably here for the baby. He won't let his child be brought up by a criminal. He'll probably want to take her when she's born.

I hold my belly protectively. I'm not giving up my baby, even if she'll have a better life with him.

Will knocks, and I open the door. "You're not taking her."

He looks confused. "What?"

"If you've come to tell me you're taking the baby when she's born, I'm telling you I won't give her up."

He shakes his head. "Can I come in?"

I pull open the door, and he steps inside. He seems too big for my tiny entryway that opens right into the kitchen.

"I can't be without you, Stella."

His hands clasp mine, and I hold my breath. "If this is some kind of trick…"

He squeezes my hands. "No. I love you. I don't care about your past. That doesn't define who you are. We've all made bad choices, and everyone deserves a second chance."

My eyes fill with tears. "But your sister?"

He winces, the pain evident in his face. "She made bad choices too. I did too. I should have come back to be with her, and I didn't."

"That's not your fault. You couldn't have known."

"We've all got things we regret in life, Stella. But one thing I don't regret is meeting you. I don't care what you were before. You're kind and beautiful, and my feelings about you haven't changed."

He pulls the ring out of his pocket. "This is still yours, if you want it."

I stare at the ring. It's too much to hope for. "Are you sure?"

He smiles, and my heart relaxes. It's the first warm look he's given me since I confessed. "I've never been surer in my life."

I hold out my finger, and he slides the ring back on.

"Just promise me you'll stop running away. We're a unit now, a family, and we'll deal with anything that comes our way together."

He pulls me into his arms, and I lean against his solid chest.

A long breath escapes me, and for the first time since I can remember I feel truly relaxed. There are no more secrets, no more uncertainty, and no more loneliness.

For the first time, I'm a part of something and I truly belong.

EPILOGUE

WILL

Two weeks later...

*T*he hired car pulls into the HQ parking lot. The familiar smell of hops hangs in the air and I breathe it in deeply, happy to be home.

I insisted on coming here first to check that the bikes had been delivered, and I couldn't wait to introduce Stella to her new extended family.

She looks nervous as I take her hand. "Don't worry. Everyone will love you."

We took our time on the road trip back, stropping in roadside motels and making love every night and in the mornings too.

We waited until Stella finished her last shift before leaving. I've been working on the road and enjoying my fiancé, sharing stories about our pasts and getting to know each other in new ways.

We've come back on the first Sunday of the month, which is when we all get together for a meal. The restaurant closes, and it's just the MC members, their old ladies and kids.

The smell of cooked meat hits me as we step through the door, as does the cacophony of noisy kids.

I grip Stella's hand tighter. She really has no idea what she's getting into. It's a big introduction to club life.

In the restaurant, the tables have been pushed together to form one long banquet table. The women are in the kitchen preparing the meal, and the men stand around drinking beers and chatting. A kid runs past, followed by a toddler trying to keep up and giggling.

All eyes turn to Stella, and the room goes quiet.

"This is Stella."

The room explodes at once, and the women come out of the kitchen. She's embraced by everyone and her belly is cooed over. I get some raised eyebrow looks over her belly.

A girl with wild hair rushes past and barrels straight into her stomach. Stella winces and catches her by the shoulder.

The girl squirms in her grasp. Her hair is tangled, and the sleeve of her top is torn.

"Sofie." Bit Rate strides over and takes the girl in his arms. She wiggles and pushes against him, wanting to be let go. "Sorry, she can't sit still."

"It's fine," Stella says.

"Daddy!" The wail comes from a small girl who looks just as wild as her sister. She tugs at Bit Rate's pants leg, wanting to be picked up. "She stole my Barbie and she pulled the head off it."

She waves a doll in the air that's missing a head. Her face is puckered up and red. "She's got no head!"

It would be funny if it wasn't so loud.

"You speak to Maxine yet?"

"Nope," he grunts. "We're fine on our own."

The other girl starts crying, and Bit Rate hustles them out of the room. He looks haggard, and I don't blame him.

Stella looks concerned, and I squeeze her hand. "Ours won't be like that, will she?"

I chuckle, because I've been around enough kids to know they can all be little devils once in a while. But she looks generally concerned.

"Ours will be a perfect angel."

She smiles, and my heart warms.

Danni bustles over and takes her by the hand and whisks her off to where a group of women are talking, wine glasses in hand.

I glance over, and our eyes meet across the room.

A warm glow fills me. I have Stella here in my club where she belongs, and I've never felt better.

* * *

WHAT TO READ NEXT

Curious about the Underground Crows MC? They get their own series!

Start with Cleo and Kray's story in His Christmas Obsession.

His obsession took him halfway across the country...

The instant I see the photo of Cleo, my brother's assistant, I know she'll be mine, with her wine-red lipstick, curvy figure, and haunted eyes.

We live over a thousand miles apart. No problem.

I'll cross the country to be with her. Hell, I'll circle the globe if it gets me to those plump lips and soft curves.

Cleo thinks I've come to visit my brother for Christmas. She doesn't know the truth. I'm not here for my brother. I'm here for her.

His Christmas Obsession is a forced-proximity, found-family, instalove steamy romance featuring an OTT, obsessed biker and the curvy woman he claims as his own.

GET YOUR FREE BOOKS

Sign up to the Sadie King mailing list and get access to all the bonus content including bonus scenes and five FREE steamy short ebook romances!

You'll be the first to hear about new releases, exclusive offers, bonus content and all my news. You can even email me back. I love chatting with my readers!

To claim your free books visit:
authorsadieking.com/bonus-scenes

If you're already a subscriber check your last email for the link that will take you straight to the bonus content.

Bad boy billionaires of the Sunset Coast and young innocent curvy woman.

His Christmas Obsession

A Christmas romance about an obsessed biker who rides across the country in the snow to reach Cleo before he's even met her.

Men of the Sea

Super short and steamy tales from Temptation Bay of bad boys and curvy girls.

Love and Obsession

A bad boy trilogy featuring a thief, a henchman and an ex-military hitman who finds redemption with his curvy girl.

For a full list of Sadie King's books check out her website

www.authorsadieking.com

ABOUT THE AUTHOR

Sadie King is a USA Today Best Selling Author of contemporary romance novellas.

She lives in New Zealand with her ex-military husband and raucous young son.

When she's not writing she loves catching waves with her son, running along the beach, and drinking good wine with a book in hand.

Keep in touch when you sign up for her newsletter. You'll snag yourself a free short romance and access to all the bonus content!

authorsadieking.com/bonus-scenes

Printed in Great Britain
by Amazon

52093513R00081